The Genius

The Adventures of Silver Dove, Book Eleven

Eliza Scalia

Cover Illustration by: Katherine Lauren
Based upon the characters originally designed by Suji Gallianetti and the further work by Wayne F. Shurtz and Cheyanne and Jean Buffkin

Dedicated to my Paul, my Tesoro. We celebrate our first anniversary this year, our paper anniversary. Paul, you have helped me through the death of a friend, the struggles of switching my career, and the problems that plague every day life. You have given me more support than I have ever had in my entire life. You try to bring joy in every moment we are together, and you are always willing to listen to my endless ideas for more stories. You are my everything, and I can only hope that I can give you the same support and love that you have provided me. It does not feel like this collection of paper is worthy of you for our paper anniversary in regards to everything you have done for me, but I know that you will see the effort and months of work I put into this and know that I have done this all for you. Everything I do is for you. I love you.

Chapter One
Colomba-
A Peaceful Day

The cold weather that had been burying my little town in snow is finally starting to disappear and the snow along the side of the roads is beginning to melt. Right now, Nat and I are walking into the school, about to start another day. It has only been three days since the Crow last attacked the school using his latest creation, the Taker. Even though it has been such a short amount of time, everyone is acting completely normal. I guess when the Crow has attacked as many times as he has, you get used to it.

Looking at my best friend Nat, I feel a wave of fear come over me as I think about the plan I have for when the Crow shows up again. It has been a bit obvious for a while that the Crow seems to have a crush on me, not as Silver Dove, but as myself. My idea is that when the Crow shows up again, I try to get him to talk to me and, with his feelings for me, he might listen to what I have to say, and I can convince him to stop doing all of this. I might be the school's only hope since everything I have done as Silver Dove has failed. I just need to wait, the problem I have is that I don't know if this is going to work. I usually ask Nonna for advice on stuff like this, but I know she would have freaked out if I told her about my plan. I am invincible as Silver Dove, but as myself I can get hurt, and there is a good chance that I could get seriously hurt doing this plan. Glancing back at Nat, I decide to swallow my fear to ask what she thinks.

"Hey Nat?" She looks at me curiously, hearing the discomfort in my voice.

"Yeah Birdy, what's up?" I take a deep breath, gathering courage so I don't back out.

"I think I have figured out something about the Crow and it is making me really nervous." She lowers her eyebrows as concern crawls across her face.

"What have you noticed?" I pause for a moment, trying to figure out exactly how I am going to tell her my crazy idea to make it sound a little less crazy, but no matter what I think of it keeps sounding crazy. Oh well, I guess I should just say it straight out.

"Well, I think that… perhaps… the Crow has a little crush on me." I look at Nat from the side of my eye, she looks a bit confused for only a moment before she bursts out laughing. I feel a bit annoyed with her, but I know that I sound ridiculous right now, so I try not to get mad. "I mean it Nat, he does." It takes a second, but she finally calms herself down enough to speak.

"Alright, alright, what makes you think that the

Crow, the evil mastermind of our school, likes you? Does he write you poetry? Is he singing you lovey-dovey songs outside your bedroom window?" Her tone is teasing me, she's not taking me seriously, I can feel my anger starting to rise again.

"I'm serious Nat, remember when the Sprinter accidentally hurt me, and the Crow carried me to safety?" Nat scoffs softly at that.

"He just felt guilty about you getting hurt, it didn't mean anything." I stop walking so that she has to stop and face me.

"There's more Nat. Whenever I get captured or cornered by one of his creatures, I get special treatment. After that monster attacked on Halloween, after the dance, the Crow showed up in my bedroom and told me that he loves me." Nat's smile immediately disappears, and absolute terror comes over her face.

"You never told me that he came to your house, how does he know where you live?" I shake my head.

"I don't know, but that really scares me. He could come to my house at any time and do something to me or my family." Nat's horror suddenly changes to confusion.

"Why didn't you tell me about this earlier? That was like two months ago." I look away from her, suddenly feeling very awkward.

"Don't you remember how everyone acted when they found out that the Crow carried me to safety when the Sprinter attacked? They treated me like public enemy number one because they thought I was working with the Crow. I was afraid that if I told you then word would get out and they would do the same thing all over again." My heart breaks at the thought of everyone treating me like an enemy again, it was so horrible to go through it the first time, I can't do it again.

"What changed though? Why are you telling me now?" I take a deep breath to try and get some courage back before I tell her the frightening answer to that question.

"Because I think that if I can talk to him, I can convince him to stop doing all this stuff as the Crow. He might listen to me if he loves me like he said he does." Nat's eyes grow as wide as saucers.

"Are you nuts? Who am I kidding? You've got to be nuts to believe that would work." My heart suddenly falls in my chest when I hear her doubt me.

"C'mon Nat, it could work." Nat scoffs at me like I am the silliest person alive.

"Yeah it'll work at getting you killed. Do you honestly think a lunatic like that would actually listen to you Birdy? As soon as you start trying to tell him what to do, he will create one of his little monsters to attack you. Tell me that he wouldn't, I dare you." I sigh softly, trying to get rid of the frustration I'm feeling right now.

"It could work Nat, he listened to me when he came into my room on Halloween. I mean he almost took off his mask in front of me, if he trusts me that much then maybe he could do this for me." Nat just shakes her head at me as if I'm being stupid for not understanding something.

"Yeah, he "almost" did, who says he would

have actually done it? Maybe he was only pretending he was about to do it to make himself look good to you. He was probably just faking it." I feel some anger rising in me for some reason when she says that he was faking this, almost as if I feel insulted that the Crow would lie to me. Why do I feel angry about this?

"He wasn't Nat, I could tell. The only reason he stopped was because he heard my dad. He would have showed me his face if my dad hadn't interrupted. He really does care about me Nat, I know it, and I can get him to listen to me. Next time he transforms someone, I will just need to approach whoever he transformed and tell the Crow that I want to talk to him. Some of the people he's transformed in the past said that he can see through their eyes when they were transformed, so I know he will see me and will know that I want to talk with him. He will make sure that his creature will keep me safe until he can come and talk to me."

"Yeah he could do that if his creature doesn't get you first. Think Birdy, think! They'll probably wipe you out before the Crow can tell them to keep you safe." Her dark eyes are full of concern, and I know that she just wants to protect me. Nat wants me to say that I will give up on this plan, but I can't. If this has a chance of working, then I need to give it every opportunity that I can to make all the horror at this school end. To keep the peace though, I know that I will need to lie to my best friend.

"You're right Nat, I don't know what I was thinking. It was just a stupid idea." I feel sick hearing myself lie to her after all the stuff we have been through together, but I know that I have to. Nat smiles at me teasingly as she lightly punches my shoulder.

"It's alright Birdy, we all go a little crazy sometimes. I'm just glad I was here to make sure you didn't do something stupid. Now c'mon let's get to class. I'm not going to let your little bit of insanity lead me to being late." Nat starts to walk away from me and into the school. Practically everyone is inside now, leaving me standing alone in the front courtyard of the school, getting chilled to the bone by the freezing wind. I walk in the school behind her, feeling very alone despite the crowd in the hallway that surrounds me.

Even though Nat may not agree with my plan and thinks that I could get myself hurt with it, I know that I need to try it. I have to try talking to the Crow and convince him to stop all this or else his reign of terror could go on forever. As Nat and I head to our first class, I try and think through exactly what I could say to the Crow when I do see him that could convince him to see things my way. When I finally make it to class right before the bell, I sit at my desk and continue to think through my plan. Nothing comes to me by the time the teacher starts class. I let those thoughts leave my mind for the moment as I pull out my pencil to start taking notes. I'm sure I will have time to think about my plan, I'm sure the Crow will wait a little bit longer to create his newest creature. I have time.

Chapter Two
Luis-
Waiting

I shuffle through the school, trying to get rid of the biting cold that I still feel even though I've been inside for an entire class period It is so cold that my fingers feel a bit numb from it. I blow into my hands to try and get some warmth in them, but it barely does anything to help me.

Walking through the hallway of the school, I am greeted by a friendly sight. Colomba and Nat are walking together as they chat cheerily. Colomba notices me and waves joyfully at me, beckoning me over. I eager go up to them and try to join in the conversation.

"Hey guys, how's it going?" The two of them are smiling at me, and it somehow makes me feel as if the entire world is warm and sunny even though it is dark and gloomy outside.

"It's going great," Nat says with a mischievous glimmer in her eyes. "Except the part where Colomba told me her "brilliant" plan on how to stop all the Crow weirdness that's been going on." Colomba glares at Nat.

"Stop it Nat, you've already teased me enough about it." She looks back at me, and then down at my hands, and her gentle eyes immediately become concerned. "Jeez Luis, your hands look freezing, you need to remember to bring gloves." I glance down at my hands, seeing that they now are a bit pink due to the cold. I look away from them, feeling a bit awkward.

"Yeah, I'm okay though, it was stupid of me to forget them." Colomba smiles softly as she takes off the scarf around her neck that I know she made herself.

"Don't worry about it, but put this on your hands for now, it will help you warm up." She wraps her scarf around my hands, and I feel like I am going to melt at her kind gesture. I smile as I look into her sweet face, wanting more than anything to kiss her to show my thanks. Instead, I am stuck with saying my thanks out loud.

"Thanks Colomba, I appreciate it. My fingers were feeling like popsicles for a second there." She smiles up at me with as much warmth as the sun.

"Of course, I'm always willing to help you." Man, I want to kiss her right now. I don't get my wish though, instead we keep walking to get to our next class. As we walk in silence, my curiosity gets the better of me, and I ask a question that I may not like the answer to.

"Hey Nat, you said that Colomba has a plan to deal with the Crow, what did she have in mind?" I say this in a teasing tone that makes Nat smile while Colomba looks a little annoyed, but more in a friendly, joking manner.

"Oh c'mon Nat, don't tell him. You already embarrassed me enough about it. Let it go." Nat just smiles at her playfully.

"Well now I have to tell him Birdy, I mean I'm probably going to need some help to make sure you don't do anything crazy." Colomba merely rolls her eyes and sighs, letting Nat tell me the secret.

"Colomba thinks that the Crow has a crush on her. So she thinks that when he shows up next time, she should try and talk him out of doing all the crazy stuff he does." My heart pounds in my chest in a panic.

"You think that the Crow has a crush on you, and you will try to make him stop?" Colomba shakes her head.

"It's not as crazy as it sounds, I mean he came to my room on Halloween and told me that he loves me, so I know how he feels, I'm sure he will listen to me." I swallow my fear as I tell her what Nat would expect me to say.

"It might seem like a good idea Colomba, but you've got to be careful. Just because he says he cares about you, doesn't mean it will be safe for you to approach him when he's doing his thing. You could get hurt by accident, so please be careful." Colomba smiles softly at me, seeing that I am being very gentle with my words and not blowing up at her like most people would in this situation. Nat doesn't show mercy though.

""Could get hurt", you mean she would definitely be hurt by that little psycho with his weird shadow dogs and giving people powers while they're having mental breakdowns. Hers is a plan that will definitely get her killed, and if you let her do this," Nat points an accusatory finger at me, "then I will make sure you don't live to see another day. Get me?" I smile as I nod at her, as if she is joking, I know she is being serious though. I know that if I let Colomba go with her plan and she gets hurt, then Nat will chase me to the ends of the earth to get revenge.

The three of us continue walking to class, talking about more pleasant subjects as we go. I smile to myself, knowing that Colomba will never have to use that plan, she will be safe. If I am going to be someone worthy of her heart, I need to be a better person and stop all the chaos I have been causing as the Crow. To do that, I am finally doing what I should have done ages ago, I am going to join Silver Dove's side and start using my powers to create peace within this world. I tried to do that by ending the bullying in my school, but I did it the wrong way. I need to be better. I can't let myself be the monster in so many people's lives. The world deserves better, Colomba deserves better, and even I deserve better from myself.

My only problem is, will Silver Dove accept me as someone she will work with? I mean just last week my last soldier made her friends and family disappear, she probably has some really bad feelings towards me right now. I'll probably need to wait a little while longer to approach her, like Shadow told me to do. Silver Dove will probably need another week or so before they even listen to me. If I tried to talk to her right now she would probably beat me up. I can't really blame her though, if someone made my family and friends disappear, I would want to beat them up to. I would deserve to get beat up for that honestly. I did a really awful thing that day, but I didn't think that would happen. I should have thought things out further, but then again, I haven't really thought anything through with my powers. I just did what I felt I should do, instead of thinking about it. That's why everything always ended in failure. I led with my heart and not my mind. If I had actually thought about it, I would have realized that Silver Dove was speaking the truth.

I let my mind get away from those dark thoughts so I can focus on the jokes Nat is telling. I just need to be patient, then I can change my life. Then I can be the better man I need to be.

Chapter Three
Colomba-
Strange Thoughts

I leave Nat and Luis behind so that I can head into my next class alone. Sitting down in my seat, I let myself relax before I start another hour of schoolwork. My mind wanders for a minute with pleasant daydreams until I hear one of the other students seated behind me stating that he is going to try and sneak into the gym when class is over. The gym is currently getting renovated and is closed off to students while they work on it. Apparently, with all the snow that we've had recently, people have noticed a few leaks in the ceiling, so they had to close it to get that sorted out. The guy doesn't explain why he wants to go into the closed gym, but I'm grateful that the guy's friend tells him to not do it, that it's stupid and he will get into trouble for no reason. Thankfully that seems to kill that stupid idea right in its tracks.

I wonder if anyone else will try to get into the gym while it's closed off. Alex apparently went in there and had taken one of the worker's wrenches to show as proof of his "brave deed". He tried to show that off to me too, but I just asked him why he would do that, it was stupid, and he stole from someone. I told him he should return the wrench, but that just made him chuckle as he told me that I needed to lighten up and stop being a buzz kill. He also said that he could show me how to really have fun in life. I could tell that he was just trying to flirt with me again, so I just told him I knew better ways of having fun besides stealing from people just doing their jobs. Alex just scoffed at that and walked away, as if I was the one being stupid and not him. I just rolled my eyes as I kept walking.

I don't understand why he thinks doing stupid stuff like that will impress me, but if I am going to believe what Nonna has told me before then some boys act stupid when they are in love. With Alex that definitely seems to be true, since he always seems to act dumb when he's around me. This guy has been chasing me ever since we started high school almost three years ago, and I haven't shown interest in him once, why doesn't he just give up and move on to another girl? There are a ton of girls who have crushes on him, he could pick any of them to date, but it seems that he has to have me. Sometimes that feels a little frightening to me, the fact that he won't give up.

Why do I just seem to attract creeps? I mean I have Alex following me, a pretty creepy guy, and I have the Crow who has a crush on me, the biggest creep in all of creep-dom… Why can't I have normal problems? I mean, I think I'm a good person, I try to do what I think is right, so why do I keep having weird stuff happen and weird guys chasing me? Why can't things just be simple?

My heart feels heavy when I realize the obvious answer to that question. I feel where the Dove Pin is pinned to my sweater, hidden underneath my jacket. I could never have a normal life if I am the one with the pin. That is what I signed up for when I accepted the pin from Nonna and took on the job of being Silver Dove. I had to give up a normal life so that everyone else can be safe and happy. That is my responsibility. And someone out there said that power has something to do with responsibility, I don't know, someone said it in some superhero movie or something.

As I sit and wait for class to start, another thought goes through my mind that instantly makes me very confused. When I had told Nat about how the Crow had come into my room on Halloween she was absolutely terrified and shocked since I had never told anybody about that. When I told Luis though, it almost felt like he already knew that, he didn't seem surprised at all. I expected Luis to overreact and ask me a ton of questions like; what happened, did he hurt me in any way, and why didn't I tell them about this before? All of those would be understandable questions for him to ask; but he didn't ask any of them. He just kept going with the conversation like it was nothing. So, did I tell Luis about what happened and then forgot about it? Did Luis just try to remain calm since we discussing something very serious? Or did Luis somehow know about what happened?

There is no way that I could forget telling Luis

something like that because he would have freaked out. I couldn't possibly forget something like that. Luis may have been trying to keep things calm, he's the kind of guy that tries to keep things chill. That may be likely. What chills my spine though is what if he already knew about it? What would that mean if Luis already knew about what happened? Would that mean that Luis knew because the Crow told him, or would it mean that Luis is the Crow? I have suspected Luis before, but stuff happened that made me think I was wrong. Was it a mistake to stop suspecting Luis, or am I just blowing this all out of proportion?

These thoughts immediately leave my mind as the teacher starts class, and I get to work, trying to take notes quickly since this teacher never stops talking so there's no time to waste or else I'll fall behind and never catch up. I don't let myself fully forget this though, I need to remember to ask Luis about this, or at least keep a close eye on him, because something doesn't feel right here.

Chapter Four
Luis-
What I
Overhear

Sitting down in my second class of the day, as everyone else is chatting and goofing off, I think about what Colomba has planned for her and the Crow. So she thinks that she can convince me to stop with my plan and make me join Silver Dove's side? She's so adorable. Too bad she will never get to try out her plan, because I'm done. I'm done with doing all the stuff everyone is so terrified of. I'm done transforming people to give them vengeance, getting revenge isn't really the best way to go anyway. I should have learned that before now with all the times I was failing with this. I always failed because of Silver Dove, but I realize now that Silver Dove was doing the right thing. I was wrong and she was right, I can't fight that fact anymore.

Now I just need to join Silver Dove's side so that we can use our powers for better things instead of just fighting each other. Problem is that I need to be patient right now. Silver Dove is probably holding on to some hard feelings towards me right now, and would most likely not want me anywhere near them, let alone try to talk to her. I mean with my last soldier the Taker, I kind of made her friends and family disappear, so I can't really blame her. I would feel pretty angry if someone did that to me too. I would probably want to destroy the world if anyone hurt Colomba, let alone make her disappear. So I just need to wait a bit longer to make sure she has let go of her anger enough to hear me out.

As I think this, I overhear someone that immediately makes me question whether or not I am doing the right thing.

"I can't believe the Crow hasn't come back yet." A guy named Carson grumbles. I don't know Carson that well, but I know that he gets made fun of a lot and is part of the Crow's fan club. These are the people who love what I do, and would love to be given powers by me so that they can get their vengeance on the world. Carson's friend Mike nods at that, looking a bit angry as well.

"Yeah I know, I can't believe he hasn't come back yet. I could probably have gotten so much more done than him if I was given those powers. That guy obviously doesn't know what he's doing. I could have made everything better for everyone here. Too bad an idiot was given the power instead." I am gripping onto the desk in front of me so tightly in my rage that I'm almost afraid that I'm going to break it in half.

Oh, so he thinks he could have done a better job as the Crow? Does he know about everything I have faced and had to deal with ever since I got these powers? Does he have any idea how hard it is to figure out these plans and then see them fall apart all because of Silver Dove? Does he know what it feels like to try so hard at something, to fail at it, and then have all of your supporters moan and groan about your failure and say they could have done better just like Carson did? Since he doesn't know that, I can tell him that it feels like you are being torn apart from the inside and nobody wants to help you in your misery. He wouldn't last a day as the Crow, nobody can. I'm the only one who can use these powers and go through these plans as well as I have. They would have given up ages ago.

I hang my head when I realize the obvious; I should have given up ages ago.

I let all of this go on for far too long. I should have joined Silver Dove's side years ago, but I let my anger control me. I kept going pretty much because I wanted to prove a point to people, but that never happened. I just made people miserable, and a sickening feeling of guilt comes over me as I think about all the people whose lives I made worse. I have hurt so many people, I don't know if the world can forgive me. When I think about how I have specifically hurt some people, if I was them, I don't think I could forgive the Crow either.

Maybe Silver Dove can help me with that, maybe if I convince her that I have changed, then she can convince the world too. She can just talk to them, probably do some kind of news interview where she can tell them this. A lot of news reporters have tried interviewing Silver Dove before this, but she always just flew away before anyone could try asking her questions. For something like this though, if I asked, I'm sure Silver Dove would be willing to tell everyone that I am on her side now. I'm sure she would, she has to. If she doesn't then the world will never accept me. I need Silver Dove since they would believe anything she said. I need her.

The final bell rings and the teacher immediately starts talking. I get out my notebook and start scribbling down what they're saying, yet not really paying attention. Now, all I can think about is whether or not the world will accept me, and if Silver Dove will even let me join her side after everything I have done. I know that if I were her, I probably wouldn't, I can only hope that she has a far more forgiving heart than I do.

Chapter Five
Colomba-
Demetrius

As I make my way through the halls, people bump into each other, almost making me feel like I am in an extreme game of bumper cars. Sometimes after making my way through the halls, I find a few bruises on myself, it can be super uncomfortable, but you can live through it.

While making my way through the crazy crowd, I feel someone bump into me. Usually, since I am so small, I feel myself move from the force of them bumping me, but this time the other person bounces off of me. Glancing over to the side, I see a familiar face, a guy named Demetrius. He is currently trying to steady himself again after bumping into me.

"Sorry Demetrius, I didn't see you there." His small body seems even smaller since he is slouching, and his head is lowered like usual so that he is looking at the ground instead of me when he responds.

"No problem Colomba, it was my fault." Just

like always, his voice is soft, almost like he is afraid to speak at a normal level. I've known Demetrius for a while now. He also works in the tutoring program that I'm a part of. Practically everyone wants him to be their tutor since they all know that he is pretty much a genius, but nobody wants to be friends with him. Demetrius is younger than any of the other students because he skipped a grade or two, so I'm guessing that he has a hard time making friends because of two things. It's hard to make friends at school when you are younger than everyone, and it is almost impossible to make friends if you're younger than everyone, yet you are smarter than them. It probably feels embarrassing trying to hang out with a guy who you would think of as a little kid, who can outsmart you in every way. I know I would be embarrassed by it, but I still try to be nice to him. Other people though, they aren't as merciful. I've heard of so many people being mean to him, making fun of him for being so smart. I honestly don't understand it. Why would you make fun of someone for being smart? Isn't being smart what everyone should strive for? Isn't being smart one of the best things you can be? Isn't that how you succeed in life? Maybe they do it because they are jealous of him? Maybe they can see that he will be successful with how smart he is, and they want him to suffer because they won't be as successful as him. So they want to bring him down to their level while they can to feel powerful about themselves right now, in this moment. Honestly, that has to be one of the most pathetic things a person can do. Dragging someone down for being amazing just so you can feel better about your normal or even pathetic life. What's wrong with those people?

I snap myself out of my thoughts when I realize I've been silent for too long.

"Don't worry about it Demetrius, you're good. How are you?" He perks up a little when he realizes that I am being genuinely friendly to him, as if this is the highlight of his day.

"I'm doing alright, how are things going with you in the tutoring program?" I chuckle as I teasingly roll my eyes.

"Well I still have to deal with Alex in tutoring, so you can guess how I feel about that right now." Demetrius laughs with me.

"Yeah, I can see what you mean, Alex does seem like he would be difficult to tutor." His tiny body suddenly starts shivering as if he just fell in a pool of ice water as he stares at something behind me with absolute terror.

"What's wrong Demetrius? Are you okay?" He doesn't answer me as I feel something wrap around my shoulders. I jump a little in surprise when I feel this, and I turn around to see Alex. My blood runs cold at the sight of him and the fury he is hiding in his eyes behind a fake smile that he directs right at Demetrius. He uses his strong arm around my shoulder to pull me in close to him.

"Yeah are you okay Demi? Or are you having trouble since I'm so difficult?" Demetrius just stares up at him like he is looking into the face of the devil. He honestly looks like he is about to pee himself in terror. He opens his mouth to try and speak, but nothing comes out, it's like his voice has been stolen. Alex loosens his grip on me for a moment so that he can lean in close to Demetrius and softly say in front of his face. "Maybe you should just leave now while I'm being nice. I don't know how long I can stay nice after what you just said." Demetrius didn't need any more warning, he pretty much runs his way through the crowd, bumping into countless people along the way in his hurry to get away from Alex. I try to go after him, but Alex tightens his grip on me, keeping me at his side.

"Hey, don't run away," Alex says to me teasingly, like I am a puppy trying to wiggle out of his grip. "C'mon, let me walk you to class. I want to talk to you about something."

"Why would you do that to Demetrius?" Alex chuckles like he didn't just threaten a guy only moments ago.

"Well he was being insulting to me Colomba, a man has to defend his honor, or whatever, right?" I push him off of me and manage to get out of his grip. I swear this guy is like an octopus with how grabby he is.

I don't even bother to give that jerk a response as I try to catch up with Demetrius. That poor kid is probably scared out of his mind and could use a friend. Problem is though, his fear must have given him wings because I can't find him at all through the crowd to save my life. Alex must have scared him really bad to make him run like that. I haven't talked to him that much outside of the tutoring program, but he has mentioned (and it's kind of obvious from how scrawny he is) but he's not very athletic, so for him to outrun me is pretty impressive.

Why does Alex have to be such a jerk to everyone? While I continue to head to my next class, I think about why Alex likes to pick on Demetrius so much, he does seem to be one of Alex's favorite targets. Alex makes fun of him a lot in the tutoring program, calling him a "nerd" and saying that Demetrius must not have a life since he seems to spend a lot of time studying and reading books. It's almost an everyday thing in the tutoring program if we are in the same room as Demetrius and whoever he is tutoring that day. Sad part is that sometimes the person Demetrius is tutoring joins in with Alex to make fun of him, which I'm guessing makes Demetrius' job a whole lot harder. I have to make Alex stop when this happens and point out to him that he may want to study as much as Demetrius does if he ever wants to pass his classes and stay on whatever sports team he is on. That usually makes him shut up pretty quick.

Actually, Alex gets embarrassed when I bring up how he needs to study more and bring up his grades, and he also seems to get upset when someone corrects him, or someone explains something to him in front of other people. Alex seems to choose his favorite people to pick on carefully. He seems to pick on Luis a lot because he is jealous that I am friends with Luis and I spend a lot of time with him. And I'm thinking he may be jealous of Demetrius too. Alex seems to recognize that one of his biggest weaknesses is that he isn't the most intelligent guy, and Alex is not the kind of person who can accept their weaknesses. He will beat the snot out of anyone who tries to point it out to him. He's probably jealous that Demetrius is smarter than him and always will be. He can probably see that Demetrius is smart and can probably do a lot of amazing things, but Alex will probably do nothing else besides the ordinary stuff that everyone does with their life. Alex knows that the smart people are the ones who usually succeed, and he's not one of them. Once high school is done, he won't be the big hero of the school anymore. Nobody will care about him and he will never have the attention he has always wanted.

Wow I just depressed myself thinking about all of that, probably shouldn't let my mind get stuck on Alex, with how mean he is he's not really worthy of my thoughts. I need to focus on more important things; like what I will say to the Crow when I see him next. It will probably take a lot of convincing for him to listen to me. Even if I do plan what I want to say now, when it happens, I probably will forget everything I thought of to say because I will be scared out of my mind. I mean who wouldn't be scared enough to pee their pants when they are around the guy who's been terrorizing their school for like three years now. Hopefully I won't do that, that would be super embarrassing to pee myself while trying to convince him to do something. I might die of embarrassment from that. I doubt I will do that though, the Crow has terrified me many times before and I haven't peed myself yet. I just need to keep telling myself that, so I won't be even more scared to talk to him.

Wait, why am I even thinking so much about how I might pee myself when I talk to him? I really need to stop being so weird in my mind, it's really not helping me and my confidence with this plan. Oh well, I will figure it out. I mean, I've got time to get this right. He hasn't attacked the school yet, so there is time. I need to just keep saying that, it will help me keep my sanity.

Sitting down in my next class, I pull out my notebook and try to get my mind to be a little bit normal so that I can focus on class. I still have a long day ahead of me, and I can't let thoughts of the Crow, Demetrius, or Alex get in the way of my own life. Opening my notebook to a blank page, I get ready to take notes, eager to let my mind be taken over by something other than my problems.

Chapter Six
Luis-
Thoughts and
Pain

Pain travels through me as I watch Demetrius run away from Colomba and Alex. From the look of terror on Demetrius' face it is obvious that Alex threatened him or something and he was running for dear life. I nearly ran over to punch Alex in the face when I saw Colomba try to squirm out of his grip, but he held on tight to her. What kind of creep will keep holding on to a girl when she obviously doesn't want to be around him? Looking at the expression on his face that clearly says "I will get what I want no matter what", I'm guessing Alex is exactly that kind of creep.

Thankfully, Colomba managed to get out of his grip before I did something stupid and confront Alex and then die far too young because of it. She runs after Demetrius, but he is too far ahead of her in the crowded hall for her to be able to catch up to him. She only runs through the crowd for a little bit before she seems to realize that it's a lost cause and just moves through the crowd like normal. Glancing behind her, I notice a strange look come over Alex. He had been smiling at Colomba with his usual grin he gives girls when he flirts with them, which is apparently super charming from what I have heard some girls say. He had smiled when he was trying to convince her to stay with him, but as soon as she got out of his grip and ran off, a dark look fell over his face and it sends a wave of anger through me. He is looking at her as if he wants to hurt her. His expression seems to scream that he is tired of being denied by her, and he doesn't want to put up with it anymore.

Alex has always gotten what he wanted, and he has always gotten the best. When it comes to the girls in this school, Colomba would definitely be the best, at least in my opinion. She is the prettiest girl by far, she is super smart, she's athletic, and most importantly she is one of the nicest people you could ever meet. For a guy like Alex, he would expect to get the best girl in the school, but he never counted on a girl not liking him back. Colomba has been telling him no since we were freshman, almost three years ago. Even though she has said no countless times, he is still trying to get her because he probably just thinks that she is playing hard to get because why would a girl turn down a guy like him? To everyone else, he is the perfect guy who deserves the perfect girl, but Colomba sees right through him, any girl with a brain would. Even though he thinks he will get her eventually after he wears her down, it hasn't worked, and it is obvious that he is losing his patience. My only fear now is what will he do to her now that he seems to be figuring out that he will never get her? Will he try to make everyone hate her like he has done to me to get revenge? Or will he do something worse; will he hurt her?

I feel my heart pound and I almost reach under my jacket to place my hand on the Crow Medal to transform myself. I stop myself, my hand only an inch away from the Medal. I didn't even think about doing that, it just happened when I thought about Alex hurting Colomba. I can't let myself do that though; for one, that would blow my secret identity, and two I can't do something to Alex just because I'm worried that he will do something when I don't know that he will actually do it. Besides, I can practically hear what Shadow would say to me if she knew what I was about to do. She would yell at me saying that I promised I would turn over a new leaf and be good and that I wouldn't use my powers to hurt people, and if I do this to Alex then I won't be any better than him. I know this, and she would be right. So, I let my hand fall back to my side as I watch Alex walk away to head to his next class. Only when I am sure that he won't turn around and do something terrible do I head to my own class.

When I get to my class and sit at my desk, I rest my head on the desk and take deep breaths, trying desperately to calm myself down. I know myself, if I let myself get any more upset about what Alex might do to Colomba then I might do something stupid as the Crow. I can't let myself do that again, I need to be better, or else I might lose myself to the hatred I am feeling. I can't do that again, never again.

Chapter Seven
Colomba-
Terrible
Thoughts

A couple of classes have passed since that little run in with Alex and Demetrius, and I haven't seen either of them since. I can only hope that I will see Demetrius later today during tutoring so that I can see if he's alright. It would kill me to find out that Alex found him later on and did something to him, trying to complete the threat he said to him. I really hope he's okay. I will need to talk with Alex during tutoring as well to tell him to stop doing stuff like that; I doubt he will listen though since I've told him stuff like that all the time. He will stop being mean to people around me, at least for a little while, but after a week or so it will start back up again. There is just no mercy in that guy's soul, he just always needs to beat people down. Alex just makes me feel exhausted sometimes having to deal with him being so obnoxious.

Thankfully, this next period is a free period for me to catch up on homework and such. Since I am all caught up on that I can relax. When I get in the classroom, I don't stop to chat with anyone, I just sit down at my desk and lay my head down to try and chill after this crazy day. I close my eyes, only planning on resting, but my body starts to feel the heaviness that tells me that I am about to fall asleep. I try to open my eyes again to wake myself up, but the sleepiness wins and instead I open my eyes to see an empty field, long grass up to my knees sways in the breeze. A beautiful spring sun brings a little warmth and comfort into this emptiness, even though in the back of my mind I know that it is actually the winter, and it is still super chilly outside. I breathe in deeply, enjoying the scent of wildflowers on the gentle breeze. I don't think I have felt this at peace since… I guess since I got the Dove Pin that turned me into Silver Dove. Ever since I pot the Pin my life has been absolute chaos and I have been super stressed since…Wow I have been depressing myself a lot today with my thoughts.

My internal conflict doesn't last long, because apparently something outside of my mind wants to cause me some trouble too. Turning around, I am staring right into the masked face of the Crow. My peace ends and I feel my heart beating like crazy as fear comes over me and I want to run in the opposite direction, but I hold my ground when I see that he isn't attacking me. The Crow is standing still, watching me with a friendly smile, a smile full of hope.

"So you want me to stop going through with my plan? You want me to stop transforming people so that I will work with Silver Dove?" I have to hold back a gasp of shock when I realize what is going on. I am seeing what will happen if I talk to the Crow like I have planned. He starts walking closer to me, and I feel my feet walking me backwards, but he is faster than me. He is slowly getting closer and closer. I should turn around and run, but I'm too afraid to turn my back on him to do so.

"You must believe in me a lot to think that I can change for the better, don't you?" He looks at me with desperate eyes behind the mask, eyes that scream that he wants me to think the best of him. As I look into that sad face, the black mask slowly seems to melt like a candle, spreading all over his face. The thing is that he doesn't seem to notice this, not even when it melts over his eyes, he still just looks at me, coming closer and closer.

"That must mean that you really care about me, don't you? Does that mean that you love me?!" In his voice I can tell that he is practically begging me to say yes. He wants me to love him more than anything. The melting mask is now covering his entire body in a black, sludgy mess. He looks more like a pile of muck than a human being. He lifts his arms out to me as if he wants to embrace me. His arms covered in the mess look like wings made of oil, like he is a bird made of slime. I keep trying to scream at myself to say that this is a dream, a nightmare, but I still feel terrified, I feel like I am about to die. I can't let him touch me with those disgusting arms that just want to embrace me.

"Do you love me? Could you love me after

everything I've done?" The sludge all over him seems to morph his body, slowly taking shape until what I see before me is a monstrous crow like creature. The thing is walking on all fours, using its wings like an extra set of legs. Long black, knife-like teeth stick out of the creature's beak while red eyes look down at me from its eight-foot height. In my surprise at seeing this thing, I don't pay attention to my feet, and I stumble backwards and fall to the ground, the grass still swaying peacefully in the breeze around me. How can this place still look so peaceful while something so terrifying is happening here?

The creature stands above me now, looking down at me like a cat about to eat a mouse it has in its paws. The blood red eyes stare at me hopefully, hoping that I will love him as well. It moves its head closer to me, its fang filled beak right in my face as it whispers one last question to me.

"Can you love me even though I'm a monster?"

I jolt up, looking around myself in terror to see that I am still in the classroom I was in moments ago. It was all just a nightmare. Thankfully nobody seems to have noticed that I had been sleeping, they are all too busy focusing on their own work or chatting with friends to notice me. I breathe a sigh of relief knowing that I won't have to deal with someone asking me what's wrong and all that, I want to be alone.

It has been a fear in my mind that the Crow might try to get closer to me if I convince him to stop with his plan and join Silver Dove. He might start thinking about me as a friend, or possibly more than friends. I would never want to date him, but if he finds that out, he might turn back to his evil ways and would probably target me with his powers. I don't even want to imagine what kind of things he would do to me or my family and friends if he got angry with me for that. I can't let that happen. I won't let it happen. I will do whatever it takes to make sure everyone is safe. If he tries to push a relationship with me, I will just tell him that I can't date him unless he proves that he won't be a villain anymore. That could take a very long time for him to do that, and maybe in that time he will lose interest in me. I can hope for that at least. Hope is all I've got at this point. All I can do is wait for the time the Crow shows his face again, try to talk to him, and hope that it all works out for the best. Opening up my backpack, I pull out a book and start reading, trying to calm my mind before I have to head to my next class. I can't let what *could* happen worry me when I already have enough on my plate to deal with now. I just have to focus on today.

Chapter Eight
Luis-
A Victim and
A Fight

My stomach grumbles, and I have to keep reminding myself that I just have one class before lunch. This is always the hardest class to get through for me. Not only is it one of my few classes without Colomba, but it's the one right before lunch so I am almost always hungry in there and the teacher doesn't let us munch on any snacks. The teacher says that we kids are too messy with snacks and will cause her room to be infested with bugs and all that. I think they're overreacting, but I doubt they will listen to me. I have to hurry though, since class is starting soon, and this teacher isn't kind to people who are late. I know that if I use these stairs there will be nobody there at this time of day and I'll be able to get to my class without any issues.

As I push through the doors into the stairwell though, I am met with a sight that makes me stop instantly in surprise and rage. Pinned to the wall by someone's massive fist is Demetrius who I can see is crying as he pleads with whoever is holding him to let him go, that he is sorry for what he said earlier today. Neither of them have noticed that I am here, they are too wrapped up in what's going on between them to notice anything else. The person who is pinning Demetrius has their back turned towards me, but I can easily tell who it is as soon as they start speaking.

"I told you to have that paper done by today, or else things would get bad for you brainiac." Alex pretty much growls this at Demetrius who looks like he is about to pee himself he is so frightened. "That paper is supposed to be turned in today, if not then I get a late grade and it will be worth less than before. If I get a bad grade on this, then I will have a hard time passing the class and I might get kicked off the football and basketball team. We wouldn't like that, now would we?" Alex smiles evilly at Demetrius, making my skin crawl and making Demetrius look like he's about to puke. It has been several hours since I saw Demetrius run away from Alex, it seems that Alex is finally getting his revenge on him for whatever Demetrius did to upset him. Demetrius opens and closes his mouth, as if he wants to speak but can't find the words for a moment before he finally finds his voice.

"W-well I j-just thought that you should do your own work, you know?" He smiles awkwardly at Alex as if trying to make the situation less bad for himself, but this just makes Alex even more furious. Demetrius stutters., knowing that he has seriously messed up. "I-I mean, I'm in all these advanced classes, right, a-and I- uh, I uh have to work a bit harder on that and it keeps me super busy, so you should be able to finish your own work, you've got more time than me." Alex laughs harshly at Demetrius, not a real laugh, but one full of fury and hate.

"Oh please, you have no idea all the stuff I've got on my plate. I have to practice and work out all the time for the teams because they all depend on me. And what do you have to do? Just read a bunch of books? That's very selfish of you, you should think about the rest of the school who would be disappointed if the team lost me and we lost all our games after that, wouldn't they? Now why don't you just finish that report by the end of the day so everyone can be happy?" Tears of fear flow down Demetrius' face as he nods his head quickly, too terrified to even speak. Alex smiles coldly at him, knowing that he got exactly what he wanted.

"Good, now get that for me before school is over, or else I might not be so nice later. Okay?" Demetrius nods at him again. Absolute panic on his poor, pathetic face. Rage boils my blood and, before I can even think, I'm stepping forward towards them.

"Let him go now Alex!" I use the same voice that I use as the Crow, deep and menacing, and Alex instantly takes his hands off of Demetrius. Terror is all over Alex's face as he turns around to face me. Somewhere deep in his mind, he recognizes this voice from when I transformed him into that monster a while back. He probably doesn't fully remember who was speaking though due to how stupid I made him when he was that monster, but it still puts terror on his face. Of course, it doesn't last when he sees that I am the one talking to him. Alex's terror instantly turns into a smile full of pride that makes me even more enraged. Demetrius is looking at the two of us, unsure of what is going on. He looks both hopeful that I might be able to rescue him or terrified that this is about to go horribly wrong. Alex chuckles darkly, as if he is about to do something truly terrible.

"Well hello there Louie, now what on earth are you doing here?" He's speaking to me like I'm a stupid little kid who has gotten themselves into a very bad situation, my rage seems to only grow every word he says.

"My name is Luis and you know it." Alex's confidence seems to crack for a second when he hears me stand up for myself, but that doesn't last long before that annoying smile comes back to his face.

"Whatever Louie, just get out of here, this doesn't concern you." Alex starts to turn around to face Demetrius again, and my rage finally boils over. This guy actually thinks that he can turn his back on me like that so he can hurt someone else right in front of me?! He thinks he can do that, and I won't do anything?!

Grabbing his shoulder, I use all my strength to yank at his shirt, to force him to turn back around and face me.

"This does concern me Al-!" I don't get to finish that sentence, because when I forced his body to turn around, he used that force to swing a punch right at my face. Pain explodes on the side of my face as he hits me square in my jaw. I practically fly off my feet from the strength of his punch and I fall in a crumpled heap on the filthy floor. I groan in agony as I try to pick myself up again. Above me, I hear Alex chuckle at me, enjoying seeing me in pain.

"You need to remember your place, Louie. Don't try to do anything like that again, or I'll make sure that the next time this happens, you will have a harder time getting back up again." I open my eyes to see him turn back to Demetrius. "Learn from his mistake, and don't keep me waiting with that paper." Alex walks away with a grin on his face, leaving the two of us alone. He leaves us feeling like our souls have just been beaten out of us. It's hard to feel like a human being when you are constantly getting pushed down into the dirt and get told that you belong there.

Even though my face is screaming in pain, I manage to get myself up on my knees to look at Demetrius. He is looking at me like he is both proud of me, as well as pitying me. He's happy that I tried standing up for him, but it's obvious that I failed. I couldn't help him. It doesn't matter how brave I was to stand up to Alex, that doesn't mean anything if you don't get any good results. Demetrius gives me a faint smile before he walks away from me, leaving me alone in the stairwell still on my knees like the pathetic *thing* that I am. When he leaves, all I can hear is the stand of my breathing echoing as I wait patiently for the pain to end. He hit me so hard in the face that I feel a little bit dizzy. It's been a while since Alex has beaten me up. With all my experience of getting hit, I know that I just need to wait a moment and I'll be able to stand again without falling over. I just need to be patient.

I know that I should be mad at Alex for hitting me, but I only feel angry with myself. Why can't I be strong enough to stand my ground against Alex? Why do I have to be so weak and pathetic? I know that I have grown a lot since I started high school, thanks to the help of Colomba and the Crow Medal, but it's obviously not enough. I was strong enough to stand up to Alex, which I would have never done a few years ago, but I'm still not strong enough to really fight back. If can't protect myself then how can I ever expect to do anything great in life if I can't even fight back against my high school bully? Is Alex right? Will I always be weak and never amount to anything in life because guys like him will always be better than me? Will I never be enough for this world?

I take a deep breath, knowing that I won't get the answers to those questions for a really long time. My face isn't hurting as much anymore, so I guess it's time for me to get off my weak butt and get on with my life. I grab my backpack and head to my next class, it's time to move on. Hopefully having a meal with Colomba after this class can help cheer me up with this dark mood hanging over my head.

Chapter Nine
Colomba-
Bruises

The cafeteria is hectic today, like normal so no big deal. People wander about with their trays of food in hand as they head to their tables to chat with their friends. I always pack my lunch, so I head straight to my usual table. I have to move around many people, practically having to squeeze past a few in the crowd to reach my table. Nat is already there with someone standing in front of the table, with their back to me so I can't tell who they are. I walk over joyfully, expecting a cheerful conversation with friends until I recognize who is standing in front of Nat, Alex. I groan softly before I continue to walk over. Now that I am closer, I can see that Nat is looking uncomfortable talking to him, looking at him as if she is silently begging for him to leave. When Nat notices me, she gives me an awkward smile, she is obviously not happy with anything going on around her right now. Nat is usually a very shy person unless she is around people she is good friends with, and being around a person like Alex would make her feel like she wants to curl herself up in a little blanket burrito and never come out. When Alex sees that she is smiling at someone, he turns around to see me approaching, and his typical, flirty smile comes over his face.

"Hey Colomba, we've been waiting for you." Yeah I bet you have, you creep.

"What do you need Alex?" I ask impatiently as I sit down beside Nat and start opening up my lunch. I try not to look at him, trying to give him a hint that I don't really care about what he has to say.

"You know that Realistic Dragon concert they're having in Socan City Saturday night? Well, guess who has an extra ticket and would love to have you come with them." I look up at him to see that he is staring at me expectantly. From the look on his face, I can tell that he expects me to get excited and say that I would love to go with him. I'm afraid I have to disappoint him.

"Sorry Alex, but I can't go, I already promised my grandmother that I would do something with her on Saturday." Alex just chuckles at that as if I am being silly.

"Oh c'mon Colomba, I'm sure you could convince your grandma to do that another day. Something like this only happens once in a lifetime." I glare at him coldly, not believing that he could say something like that. He expects me to change plans with my own family just to go on a date with him even though I have always refused to go on a date with him every single time he has asked before. I roll my eyes at him as I try to calm myself down, so I won't yell at him in front of everyone in the cafeteria.

"No Alex, I'm not doing that. Plus, I don't even like that band, so I'm not interested in going. Just take one of your friends with you, I'm sure they will enjoy it more than me." Alex leans in closer to me, like he wants to tell me an important secret. With him standing over me, it almost feels like he's trying to keep me trapped in this spot until I give in to what he wants.

"Colomba, you know that there's no one else on earth that I would rather go with than you." He rests his hand on top of mine. With his massive hands pretty much covering my tiny ones, I feel even more trapped. I feel my heart start to pound in panic. It takes a little bit of struggle, but I manage to get my hand out from under his.

"That's sweet Alex, but I really don't want to go. I have other plans and I am sticking to them. Please just leave, I won't change my mind." A flash of anger passes over his face for only a second before his usual fake charming smile replaces it. When that look of anger was on his face for that moment, I almost felt like running. That anger was something that truly frightened me. That looked like the anger of someone who could hurt someone. I almost let out a sigh of relief when he let his usual grin return.

"Alright, I'll give you until tomorrow morning to change your mind." He gives me a little wink that tells me that he thinks I will change my mind and come crawling back to him, begging him to let me go on a date with him. I can only give him a straight face as I give him my response.

"Don't worry Alex, I won't." Alex keeps the

smile on his face, but fury burns in his eyes, and I want to shrink at the sight of it. I want to be able to hide from that rage. I actually do let out a sigh of relief when I see someone coming to my table that I know will help me feel better in this crazy situation.

"Hi Luis." I wave at him, smiling joyfully at my savior, and Luis gives me a warm smile back as he sits down beside me, getting in between Alex and me. Did I see it wrong, or did Alex look concerned when Luis came close to me? Why would Alex be uncomfortable with this? He knows that Luis and I are friends and have been for ages; so what's bad about us hanging out at lunch and sitting next to each other? I get my answer as soon as Luis looks at me and I can clearly see his face. One of his cheeks is a dark purple due to a huge bruise that pretty much covers the lower left side of his face. Due to my experience with martial arts, I can easily tell that Luis has been punched in the face. I've seen this wound many times, and it is always saddening to see since you can tell that person is in a lot of pain. Luis is trying to hide that pain from me, but I can see it, he is trying to be strong. All of that is obvious to me, but there is one thing I don't understand that I need to know more than anything.

"Luis, who did this to you?" I gesture towards his face, and Luis doesn't even have to say anything to give me his answer. He just looks up at Alex, and when I see the panic on Alex's face I understand. Glancing down at Alex's right hand, I see the only other bit of evidence I need to realize what must have happened. Cuts are on Alex's knuckles, similar to what I have seen in my martial arts class when someone has punched something too hard and possibly hit it in an incorrect fashion. I stand up from my chair, getting right up in Alex's face.

"How could you do this Alex?! What kind of monster are you?!" Alex looks at me with absolute terror, as if he can't believe I figured out what happened so quickly. He tries to hide that terror by switching his expression to make himself look shocked at my outburst.

"What are you talking about Colomba? I didn't do this." He sounds so confused right now that if I didn't see the evidence right in front of me, I might have believed him. With Luis glaring at him with enough hatred to make my skin crawl, I see right through his lie.

"Don't lie to her Alex, she's smart enough to see that you did it." Alex turns his attention to Luis, surprise making his eyes grow wide as if he can't believe that Luis said that, that Luis was able to stand up for himself. His surprise quickly melts into fury as he practically growls at Luis.

"Shut up Louie, this doesn't concern you!" I step in between them so that Alex won't try to do anything else to him.

"His name is Luis, not Louie, so show some respect. And also, this does concern him since it was *his face* that you punched!" Alex turns his attention back to me, his rage directed at Luis immediately morphs into a pitiful expression as soon as he sets his eyes on me.

"I swear Colomba, I didn't do it. He's just blaming me because he has always hated me." I know that Luis and Alex do not like each other, I would have to be blind to not see that, but Luis is too kind and honest of a person to blame Alex for something like this. Luis would never lie to me, Alex on the other hand always seem to have some lie to use just in case things aren't going his way. Plus, Alex seems to always have more hatred towards Luis for some reason even though Luis doesn't seem to do anything to Alex except try to fight back when Alex does something mean to him. I don't know where or when their hatred started, but this is going too far because in a physical fight there is no way that a lanky guy like Luis could ever win against a strong guy like Alex. It is an unfair fight, and even someone as dense as Alex can see that. I just roll my eyes at Alex, wanting nothing more than to yell at him in front of everyone in the cafeteria, to embarrass him, but I keep a cool head and just glare at Alex with a stern expression.

"I don't care about your lies Alex, just go away and never talk to me again. I don't want to be around a monster like you." Alex starts begging to try and tell me that I'm wrong, that he can explain, but I don't pay attention. Instead, I pull out the ice pack I keep in my lunchbox to keep my food cold so that Luis can put it on his cheek. Luis smiles when I do this, flinching a bit as he puts it on his cheek due to the pain.

As Luis smiles at me, from the corner of my eye, I can see Alex's pathetic expression quickly morphing into something frightening, something so full of hatred that I want to cower from him like a frightened child. At first that rage is directed at Luis, but his eyes shift to look at me as Alex points an accusatory finger at me, as if he is about to blame me for a terrible crime.

"You will regret this Colomba, you will regret choosing him over me. Why would you even want to be around a pathetic little freak like him, when you could have me instead?" Even though I am afraid, I look him in the eyes so I can give him the answer he doesn't want to hear. I try to keep my voice steady, even though I feel shivers of fear going through me.

"I would rather be around someone who actually has a heart Alex, someone who isn't kind just so they can get something from me. I only want people in my life who truly care about me, not ones who are obsessed with me and never leave me alone even when I tell them to. Now just leave us alone." Alex's hands tighten into fists at his side, and for a split second I'm afraid he is going to hit me too. Luis must have noticed this too since I feel him tense up beside me, as if he is getting ready just in case Alex tries to start something.

Alex must have seen the fear come across my face since he instantly relaxes his body, and his fists loosen. With a horrified expression, Alex looks down at his fists, realizing what he could have done. He looks back up at me as if he has finally realized that I was telling the truth, that he is the monster right now. Without another word, Alex slowly turns around and walks away, the only good decision he has made in the last few minutes we've been talking.

Only when he is far away from our table do I let out a deep breath that I didn't realize I had been holding in my fear. Looking at Nat and Luis, I can see that Nat had been terrified too, but Luis' face holds a much darker emotion. In his eyes, I see even more hatred than I had seen in Alex's face, in his eyes I see murder.

"Luis, you okay?" My soft words seem to snap him back into reality and he gives me an awkward smile, like he just got caught doing something terrible.

"Yeah, I'm alright. What about you Colomba? What was he trying to do this time before I showed up? He wasn't doing anything sketchy right?" I can't help but smile at his words, even with everything that happened, and even though Alex punched him in the face earlier today, he's still more concerned about me than himself. He is such a sweet guy. I'm so lucky to have a friend like him.

"It's alright, I'm fine, nothing happened." I try to smile back at him, but even I can tell that my smile is pretty weak. I can't hide the negative feelings I have inside. Luis' eyes narrow and I can feel his worry and anger come through. He looks away from me to look at Nat.

"Nat, Colomba's lying isn't she?" I turn to face Nat, silently begging her not to tell him anything. I don't want him to feel worse than he already does. Nat lowers his eyes away from my pleading gaze before she turns her attention to Luis.

"Alex came over here before Colomba sat down, asking me where she is, and he wasn't nice about it either. He was pretty much demanding me to tell him where she is. When she showed up, he turned on the charm and tried to ask her out, but she said no. He kept pushing her to go with him no matter what she said. Then you showed up and it all hit the fan from there." Even though Luis doesn't say anything, I can tell that what Nat said just made him a lot more angry. I glare at Nat and mouth the word "traitor" to her. She looks down at her hands in discomfort, knowing that I'm right and that she caused him more pain. Resting a hand on top of Luis', I try to comfort him as best as I can.

"It's alright Luis, we're both fine. And I'm sure that after all this he won't come anywhere near us again. You don't have to worry about us." I can still feel the tension from his anger in his hand. Judging from the look of pure rage on his face, I don't think he even heard a word I said. He looks like he is trapped within his mind, stewing in his fury as he thinks about what happened. I gently squeeze his hand, and this seems to snap him back to reality. He looks over at me with surprise, almost like he forgot I was here. Luis gives me a gentle smile, but one that I can see is forced, he doesn't feel any better, he probably feels worse.

"Alright Colomba, please just tell me if he starts bugging you again. I don't want you to be afraid like that ever again. With how he has always acted towards you, I doubt he will stop now. You've turned him down countless times before, and he always comes back. Please, please tell me if he tries anything again." He squeezes my hand gently, like how my dad used to when I was little and upset. His eyes are pleading with me, begging me to be careful with Alex, wanting me to be safe more than anything. This brings a smile to my face, and I look deeply within his eyes, hoping and praying that everything will be okay.

When I look into his eyes though, I have a feeling that things are about to get a whole lot worse. Within his dark eyes, I see a hatred that he is trying to hide from me. Within his eyes, I see something that I know I should be afraid of, but looking at my friend, I can't be afraid of him. I could never be afraid of someone who is as kind and gentle as Luis. He would never harm me, so I should not be afraid of him. When I look into those eyes though, I have the feeling that something terrible is about to happen, and my dearest friend will be the one to blame for it. I know that he would never harm me, but that doesn't mean he won't harm anyone else. And I have a deep, dark feeling that people are going to get hurt, especially a specific person in this school who Luis is still glaring daggers at as they make their way to the other side of the cafeteria to sit with their friends who are considered the popular sporty people. From over there, Alex joins in the conversation, but as I try to enjoy my lunch, I catch him sneaking looks over at me, and not all of those looks are positive. I feel as if I am being watched under a microscope that I can never escape from, while Luis seems to be observing me in the same way, but his gaze is far kinder. His gaze is trying to determine if I am really alright. I don't know if I can hide it from him, but I am not okay, and I will not be okay, not until I finally feel safe.

Chapter Ten
Luis-
Changes to
Be Made

Just Lunch has passed, and my next class has already started, but the fury I feel has not died down. Tapping my fingers on my desk impatiently, I need to wait until I find a good moment to ask to go the bathroom. I need to be alone for what I have to do. Since it is English class, the teacher talks to us about the book we are reading and then tells us to read the next chapter until class ends. Thankfully, I have already finished that chapter. I go up to the teacher's desk to tell her this, and then ask to go to the restroom. She says yes, and I am out the door like a flash of lightening.

In the silence of the halls, my stomping feet seem to echo all across the school. It doesn't take long for me to find a bathroom. Looking around carefully, I make sure that I am alone before I lock the door and place my hand on the Crow Medal. Shadow appears on the counter beside me, but I don't even bother to say hello. I have work to do.

"Shadow, you've got to transform me into the Crow, right now." Shadow cocks her head to the side in confusion as she stares up at me with her dark eyes examining me carefully.

"Why Luis? What on earth would you need your powers for at a time like this?" I almost feel like laughing at her, the answer is so obvious.

"Because we need to transform Demetrius, that's why. He should get powers just like everyone else. You saw how they were treating him, he deserves it." Shadow shakes her head slowly at me.

"Are we really going through this again Luis? You have tried and failed so many times before. What makes you think this time will be any different?" It takes me a minute to speak, I was so stunned by her words to think of an answer for a second. Shadow is so blunt with me sometimes, makes me feel like I'm getting slapped in the face with her cruel honesty sometimes.

"He will be different because he's smarter than anyone else in this school. He will be able to plan against Silver Dove more affectively. He can succeed because he will be smart enough to realize that I am right, and that Silver Dove is just lying to him. He will see it!" Shadow just stares up at me in silence, as if she is trying to figure out whether I'm joking or not. I keep my face as deadly serious as possible so she knows that I mean business. After a minute of us just staring at each other, she lets out a faint sigh as if in defeat.

"I thought you had said that you wouldn't do this anymore. You said that you would finally join Silver Dove's side and do what you are meant to do, bring peace to this world. Or are you just doing this because of how Alex was treating Colomba? You had an entire class period in between what happened with Demetrius and what happened in the cafeteria; why wait until what happened with her if you are doing this for Demetrius? Or are you hoping this will change things between you three and she will be free of Alex?" I glare at her, my fury boiling over.

"She has nothing to do with this!!" For a split second I worry that someone in the hall may have heard me yell that, but I'm too angry to let that thought stay in my head long. Shadow just shakes her head at me like she is a parent who is disappointed by their child.

"She always does. Colomba has been your motivation for everything you have done as the Crow." She sighs softly, her beaked face lowering as if she is too saddened by me to even look at my face. "You said that the Taker would be your final one, that you would finally end this madness and fulfill your destiny with the Crow Medal." I lower my gaze away from her, feeling a bit ashamed with myself. I did tell her that I would do all that, I can't lie to myself and say I didn't. I will admit that teaming up with Silver Dove was starting to sound tempting, but this opportunity with Demetrius doesn't present itself every day. He could be the one to complete my mission. I look back up at Shadow, trying to look as confident and reassuring as I possibly can.

"It's okay Shadow, this will be the last time. If Demetrius fails then I won't do this again and I will join Silver Dove's side, I promise. Just one more time, that's all I need." Shadow's pitying, compassionate stare immediately switches to a merciless, chilling glare as her feathers fluff out a little in silent fury.

"And how many other "one last times" will there be before you realize this won't work out?" She doesn't give me time to answer that question, since she takes off into the air and starts flying around me faster and faster. I know what she is doing. I close my eyes for only a moment, and when I open them again, I have been transformed into the Crow. Turning to look at myself in the mirror, I see the Crow, but it doesn't feel like myself today. Closing my eyes, I let myself relax, knowing that this time, I might have a happy ending with this.

"Shadow, find Demetrius." I feel Shadow pass by me like a faint breeze and head underneath the door and out into the hallway. She flies past classroom door after classroom door until she finds the one she needs. Slipping under the door, she finds Demetrius sitting in the front of the class, taking notes like the good student he is. Shadow flies straight into his heart right as the bell rings, signaling the end of class, and Demetrius starts putting stuff away. When Demetrius has put away his notebook and other stuff away, I make myself known to him.

Demetrius.

Demetrius jumps a little in his seat and looks around, absolutely terrified, but nobody pays attention to him.

Act natural Demetrius, get your stuff and start walking to your next class like nothing is going on. We have some things to talk about.

Demetrius does as I say, and steps out of the classroom, joining the crowd going in every direction to get to their next class. Thankfully, Demetrius is smart enough to realize who I am without going through the usual questions people ask when I start talking to them through their minds. He also realizes that since I am in his mind, then he can talk to me the same way.

What do you want from me, Crow? Are you going to transform me like you've done to those other people?

You catch on quickly, that is exactly what I have in mind. You've always been seen as intelligent, but I can make you more than that. I can make you the most intelligent person who has ever lived. I can make it so that you can change the world for the better and make sure that nobody will ever bother you again. With a mind like that you can defeat Silver Dove with ease, then you can live a life without fear of people hurting you again. What do you say?

I feel Demetrius' lips pull up into a sly smile as

he slips into a janitor's closet so that he can do what he needs to.

Give me the power, I'll make you proud with what I can accomplish.

I don't even give him a response, it isn't necessary. Instead, I just let Shadow's power invade him like a virus. It easily goes through his willing body until his transformation is complete. When he is done, I let myself fade as the Crow until I am back to my usual self. I need to let myself be seen by others so that no suspicion will fall on me. Plus, I just want to see firsthand what my newest soldier will do.

Chapter Eleven
Colomba-
I Sense
Danger

I carry my books through the halls, trying to get to my last class for the day. Today has been so frustrating with everything that happened with Luis and Alex at lunch. How could Alex do that to Luis? I swear, sometimes Alex just acts like a stupid ape, just using his muscle to get whatever he wants. Luis explained what happened between them and Demetrius. Over an hour has passed since Luis told me about it, and I'm still so mad about it all. I couldn't even pay attention in my last class because I couldn't get that out of my mind.

Luis tries to stand up to Alex to defend Demetrius and gets punched in the face for it. I stand up to Alex all the time, but he just laughs it off and tries to flirt with me. I know he does that because I'm a girl and he wants to date me, but it's still so annoying. Why can't he just leave Luis and I alone? I've told him I'm not interested so many times, but he still chases after me.

Honestly, I have no idea why he is always using Luis as a target for his cruelty either. Ever since I have known the two of them, they have been at each other's throats. I will admit though that Alex always seems to be the one starting things and gets Luis upset, while Luis just responds to Alex, usually in a really angry manner. What started all of this between the two of them? I've tried asking Luis about it a couple times, but he never gave me an answer, he always tries to change the subject. I never push him to give me an answer, but I really want to know. I do have a feeling though that having me around has only made things worse between them. It's obvious that Alex likes me, and having Luis as my best friend just makes Alex crazy with jealousy. With how Alex acts sometimes, it makes me think that he really is crazy sometimes.

My life as Silver Dove is already crazy enough as it is, having all this go on in my regular life is just getting to be too much. Sometimes, I just want to take a nap and forget about all the stuff I have to deal with, but I have too much on my plate to let myself rest like that. When I'm at school I have my advanced placement classes, all the drama with my friends right now, watching out for signs of the Crow, working in the tutoring program, and just trying to stay on top of all my work. When I am at home I have my chores, training with Nonna as Silver Dove to make sure I am as powerful as I can be for whenever I have to face the Crow again, martial arts practice, working on homework, and trying to finish needlework projects with Nonna so that we can sell them to people. It feels like I never have a break, but I know I can't let myself rest, not until the Crow is no longer a threat. Only then can I have peace in my life.

As these depressing thoughts run through my head, a familiar feeling comes over me, and my heart starts racing when I realize what that feeling is; it's the signal that the Dove Pin gives me whenever something bad is about to happen. I turn my head in the direction of where the Pin is telling me the danger is coming from, and I see that I am facing the door to the gym. Spread across the door to the gym is a sign that says "Do Not Enter: Under Renovation", but I don't pay attention to that. Taking a deep breath, knowing that the Crow could be the danger hidden behind this door, I prepare myself for what needs to be done. I will talk to him, I will make this end so we all can finally have peace. This could all be over very soon. Pushing the door open, I enter the gym.

Chapter Twelve
Luis-
The World Transformed

Wandering through the hallways, trying to not get bumped into by every single person in this school, I wonder what is going on. The hallways are crowded, full of noise, people, and activity, but everything seems normal. What is going on? What is my soldier doing with the power I've given him? Is he even using it? Every other time I have given someone powers, they never took this long to do something; they're usually doing something right after they figure out how to use their powers. This guy should be smart enough to know what he needs to do to get the vengeance he wants and to change the world the way he sees fit.

A weird, uncomfortable feeling comes over me, like a heavy rock has just been dropped in my stomach, and I instantly know what it means. My soldier is close, and I should probably go see him to see what is going on. Looking around, I try to figure out where this feeling is leading me, and it doesn't take long before my eyes fall onto the gym doors. A huge sign says that nobody is allowed inside the gym because of the construction going on in there, but I don't care. Glancing around to make sure nobody notices me, I slip silently through the doors, trying to mentally prepare myself for whatever may hide behind these doors.

When I get in the gym, I am instantly greeted by a strange sight. My newest soldier is standing in front of a massive machine the size of a shed that is creating weird noises as many lights on it blink on and off while my soldier walks all around it, observing it like it is an alien species he is fascinated by. Before he can notice me, I jump behind the bleachers and silently have Shadow transform me into the Crow before I step out to speak to him.

"Soldier, what are you doing?!" My soldier slowly turns his head towards me for only a moment before returning his gaze to his work. Strange, whenever I address my soldiers they usually give me their undivided attention and act a bit afraid of me. He isn't afraid though, not even a little. He is acting like he is just talking with a friend. Why is he so relaxed right now?

"Don't worry Crow, I am doing exactly what I said I would do. I am creating a better world. I am creating a world where the intelligent will be the most powerful. I will make it so that throughout all of history, the most intelligent will have been the ones ruling the world, not the strongest. Intelligence will be the most important thing a person will have. Once I press this button, everything will change." My soldier points at a large green button next to him, and I feel my heart start to race at the sight of it.

"I don't understand." My soldier only chuckles at me.

"Of course you don't Luis, you aren't intelligent enough to see what could be." My heart had been racing a moment ago, now it feels like it is going to explode in my chest. He knows who I really am?! He finally looks away from my work to smirk at me. "Yes, I know who you are beneath that mask. With the power you have given me, it wasn't that hard to figure out. Don't worry though, if I have judged you correctly, you will be living a much better life within my new world." A squeaking sound makes the two of us turn our heads to see that someone just entered through one of the doors on the other side of the gym. My pounding heart freezes when I see that it is Colomba, who is looking from me, to my soldier with his massive machine, and then back to me. When her eyes rest on me, she looks at me with an expression of terror as well as hurt.

"You're already doing this again Crow? It hasn't even been a week since the last time." I move a few steps closer to her, but stop when I see her flinch in fear.

"Colomba, please I-" She just shakes her head at this, looking irritated with me.

"No Crow, there are no excuses, you need to stop this now! Stop this before it's too late! Whatever he is doing, stop him before anyone gets hurt!" Even though she says that other people could get hurt, when I see her, all I can think about is what happens if she gets hurt. I turn to my soldier, anger flaring up inside me. I open my mouth to speak but he interrupts me before I can even start.

"Don't worry Crow, my machine will not harm the love of your life." He grins mischievously at me when he calls Colomba that. "Get ready for my new world." Before I can do anything else, I see him reach for the green button. Knowing that I am too far away to stop him from pressing the button, I do the only thing my heart is telling me to do. Protect Colomba. Lunging towards her, I grab her, holding her tightly in my arms, as my black wings wrap around us, shielding us from the blinding green light that seems to explode from the machine beside us. I hold her close to me as we both fall to the ground from the force that the machine created with that light. We land with me on top of her while it feels like a tornado is blowing all around us. It only lasts for a moment before everything is suddenly calm and I hear an annoyed voice speaking beneath me.

"Luis?! What are you doing?! Get off of me!!" Opening my eyes, I see Colomba lying on the ground beneath me, anger burning in her eyes. Something is different though, she is wearing different clothes. She had been wearing a sweater with pants a second ago, and now she appears to be wearing some kind of school uniform. She is wearing a dark blue sweater vest over a white collared shirt with a black pleated skirt. White stockings cover her legs while fancy looking black leather shoes cover her tiny feet. Her beautiful hair is held back by a dark blue ribbon that matches her sweater vest.

I quickly hide my confusion as I get off of her, and hold my hand out to help her up, but she gets up on her own, purposefully ignoring my extended hand. I bring my hand back, feeling super awkward. Colomba brushes herself off, still looking irritated with me.

"Hey, I'm sorry Colomba, I didn't mean to knock you down like that." Colomba just rolls her eyes at me.

"Yeah, sure you didn't." she practically growls at me in annoyance and frustration. Without another word she walks away from me, towards the exit of the gym, leaving me standing here wondering what is going on. I start moving towards her, to try and catch up to find out why it looked like Colomba almost hates me, but I stop though when I see my reflection in a glass window. Not only had Colomba's clothes changed, but I have changed too. I am wearing a uniform similar to Colomba's. I am wearing a dark blue sweater over a white collared shirt with black pants. What really catches my eye though is that my hair is different. Usually my hair is long, hanging in my face like I am trying to hide from the world. Now though, my hair is cut short so that my face is clearly seen.

My mind instantly realizes what could have caused this major change, and I look behind myself to look at the machine my soldier had made, but there is nothing there. All there is behind me is a very clean, but rather empty gym. There isn't the usual gym equipment here, just the bare minimum, as if the school could care less about this room or gym class. That's weird, this room is usually full of stuff for people, especially the sports teams, to work out with. What is going on?

I hear the door to the gym open up, and I see a quick glimpse of Colomba before she walks out the door and out of my sight. Panic suddenly floods through me, and I rush towards the door, not wanting to lose the only person I feel like I can trust in this new world. Running towards the door, I practically rip it open, hoping to find Colomba, and instead I am stunned by what I see.

The school looks barely like the one I left behind, every single thing is different. Everything looks better than what I left behind. The halls are crowded with students in uniforms, talking quietly with each other. Everything is spotless and clean, and I can see that it's so clean because of a few small robots that are patrolling the hallway and cleaning up anything that they see as even remotely dirty. Large screens show stuff from all over the world, from stock market stuff, historical documentaries, and scientific debates.

I start walking through the crowd, trying to look normal in this strange crowd. I see familiar faces, but they all are wearing these uniforms and they all look a lot more neat and tidy than they have before. As I continue to watch people, I notice something else that makes this world seem even more strange.

All of the people who were the sports stars and popular people in my old school aren't acting like they used to. They used to hold their head up high with pride, but now their heads hang in despair. A few people that used to get made fun of for being part of the nerdy crowd, pass by the people who were popular in my world and laugh at them. The nerdy people throw insults at them, mocking them for not being intelligent, while the people who used to be popular just cower away from the nerdy group. What is going on here? If this had happened before, the popular guys from the sports teams would just beat up the nerdy guy for even trying to insult them. They would make sure that the nerdy guy is so terrified of them that they won't even look at the popular guy as they pass each other in the halls.

As I continue watching the guy who used to be a popular sports star who was just got mocked by the nerds, walks past a group of girls and they giggle as he looks at them as he passes by. I hear them whisper about how he is such an idiot and that he shouldn't even be looking at them since they would never date an idiot like him.

What on earth did that machine do? My soldier said that his machine will change the world we live in, that it will change history to make intelligence the most important thing a person could have. As I look around, I know that his machine worked. He didn't send me to a new world, this is my world, but with history changed.

My horror when I realize this quickly fades when a few people, who never would have talked to me in the old world, say hi to me with friendly smiles. I say hi back, feeling a bit awkward, but they move on their way, not laughing at me or anything... You know, this world might not be so bad after all. I think I could like it here.

I head to my next class with a smile on my face. A few more people greet me along the way, and when I get to the classroom, some more people greet me there and they eagerly invite me to join in their conversation. I think that this soldier may have finally figured out how to improve the world in a way I never could. I think I may have finally won, I can finally be happy.

Chapter Thirteen
Colomba-
Something is Different

I head to my next class, still fuming about Luis falling on top of me like that. Who does he think he is doing something like that? I stop walking for a moment as I realize something; what were we doing in the gym together? Why did he fall on top of me like that? What was going on there?

Looking around the hallway, a strange feeling comes over me, is something different? All around me I see the people I usually see in their uniforms, the janitor robots cleaning, and the big televisions all along the wall showing news and other stuff from around the world. Everything is just like it always is, so why does it all suddenly feel so strange? And why do I have no memory for why Luis and I were doing in the gym a few minutes ago?

I shake my head a little, as if that will shake those thoughts out of my brain. It was probably nothing, I have bigger issues at the moment. I have a big test in my next class that I need to focus on. I've been studying for this for ages, and I can't let myself get distracted now. I try to get my mind to focus on the stuff the test will discuss, but I can't help but think about what was going on in the gym. Why can't I remember it? This is really freaking me out!

Stepping into my next class, Nat waves at me with her usual cheerful grin on her face. I try to hide my annoyance and confusion, putting a smile on my face to make sure I don't worry her.

"Hey Nat, what's up?" When she hears my voice, concern immediately goes across her face. Her dark eyes narrow as she examines me.

"What's wrong?" I try to look like I have no idea what she's talking about, but I know I can't hide from her. I still try anyway though.

"What do you mean?" She rolls her eyes at me like I am trying to play a prank on her, but it's obvious what I'm doing.

"C'mon Birdy, tell me, was Luis bugging you again?" I sigh, knowing that the game is over.

"Yeah, yeah he was." Nat groans in annoyance.

"Jeez, that guy doesn't know how to take a hint. I mean he's a smart guy and is pretty cute, but just because he has that doesn't mean that you will fall into his arms. How long has this guy been trying to get you to go out with him?"

"Ever since the first day of our freshman year when we met." Nat just shakes her head at that.

"Dang, you think most guys would move on by that point, but, of course, not Luis. A guy like him always gets what he wants. He should just go after some other girl. I pity whoever that next girl will be." I know that Nat is completely right about how Luis should just move on, but I also can't help but see that many girls in school would be happy to be in a relationship with him. He is a handsome guy, very charming, intelligent, and one of the best artists I have ever seen. I can understand why so many girls have a crush on him, he is a catch, but not for me. I have seen too much of who he truly is to ever be interested in him. I don't even want to think about it.

I get in my seat as the teacher goes to the front of the room to start class. I will do well on this test, I know it, but I can't let my focus be on Luis. He doesn't deserve my time or thoughts. When the teacher hands me my test paper, I let my eyes scan the page, ready to get this done and over with. While I look over the pages, I can't help but think about what happened in the gym again, and why I can't remember it. Did I hurt my head and that affected my memory, or did Luis do something terrible and then did something to me to make sure I wouldn't be able to remember what it was? I don't know, but my spine tingles at the thought of what that awful guy could have done.

Chapter Fourteen
Luis-
Good Changes
Bad Changes

Today has to be one of the greatest days of my life. All day, everyone has been acting like I am their friend, not the guy they make fun of all the time. People actually want me to sit with them and tell me all about their plans for the weekend, they even invite me to come with them to go shopping, go to do activities, and even go to parties. I have never had anything like this happen in my life. I actually feel like I am here, that people can see me and accept me. What my soldier has created here has to be the most perfect world I could have thought of.

It is weird how Colomba treated me earlier though. I've never had her get mad at me before, I'll admit it really hurt seeing her get so angry at me. It was strange, but I guess in her view I had fallen on top of her for no reason and that probably hurt a lot, so she will probably stop being mad at me by the end of the day. She never stays mad at anybody for long, she's too sweet of a person to do something like that. I just need to find her and apologize, and then all will be perfect. I'm heading to my next class now, and hopefully she will be there too.

Turning around a corner, I am surprised to see a crowd surrounding something. They are all laughing at something while someone in the center of the group is yelling insults at someone; calling them an idiot and saying they will never get anywhere in life. I make my way through the crowd easily. Usually, I have to squeeze and push a little to get through crowds, but since I am very popular in this world, people let me by. When I make it closer to the center of the crowd, I finally see who they are laughing at, and I almost can't believe my own eyes. Alex is cowering away from a guy who used to be considered one of the biggest nerds in the other world. Now, the nerd is throwing insults at Alex while Alex looks like he is about to cry.

"Why would you ever think that I would waste my time helping a moron like you with homework?! Teaching you would be useless since you don't even know the basics for anything! The only reason you got into this school was because your dad paid extra to let you in with your terrible grades! You are pathetic, and with how stupid you are, you will never make it in this world!" I feel like my heart is about to burst with joy. I can't believe I am seeing this. I have dreamed of watching something like this for years, almost my entire life, and now here it is. I have got to take advantage of this moment before it's over. I can't let it go to waste.

Stepping through the crowd, I pull a water bottle out of my backpack and unscrew the top of it. Alex looks up when he notices someone coming closer to him. For a split second, there is a look of hope in his eyes as if he thinks the person approaching him will help him, but when he sees that it is me, absolute fear comes over his face. It is beautiful. I need to remember this look on his face for the rest of my life. In his face I can see a lot about the life I must have led in this world that I don't know. In his face, I know that I really am a popular guy around here, and I know that I am someone who picks on Alex a lot, and I'm glad about that. I wonder if my soldier knows how much I got bullied in the old world by Alex and decided to let me be his bully instead in this world. If he did, I love him for that.

"Here Alex, maybe adding a bit more water to your diet might be able to improve your brain function. Although with your tiny brain, you would need to drink the entire ocean to fix yourself, but it's a start at least."

Nobody says anything, and nobody does anything to stop me as I pour the entire water bottle on his head. The water trickles down his face and all over his clothes, soaking almost his entire upper body. The entire hallway erupts into laughter and applause as I do this, and I feel as if all of the hatred I have felt for him for all of these years has finally been satisfied. It's like a huge weight has finally been taken off of me, and I can finally breath for the first time. Looking at the crowd around me, everyone is cheering me on, everyone is throwing insults at Alex as if they think he is the most disgusting, pathetic creature on earth. I can't believe I am seeing this.

When I look back at Alex though, everything

changes in an instant. In his eyes I see complete misery. In his eyes I see that he knows that he can't fight back against me, or else things will be worse for him. In his eyes I see absolutely no hope, he believes that his entire life will be just as terrible as this moment. In him, I see defeat.

I know exactly what that feels like.

I have felt that so many times in my life; every single time someone picked on me I felt that way. I have felt that and hated that feeling, and now I have made someone else feel this way. What have I done? My heart feels like it is being crushed in my chest. What am I doing? Why am I doing this? As I keep looking at him as the crowd continues to laugh, I remind myself that this is Alex, the guy who constantly hurts me in my old world. I shouldn't feel sorry for him after everything he has done, but I can't help it. Even though I know the kind of person he is, I can't help but feel terrible for what I have done.

I'm surprised when a familiar figure comes out of the crowd, but they aren't joining the fun like everyone else. Instead, they go straight over to Alex, who smiles at them as if they are looking at their savior. They rest their hand on Alex's shoulder in a comforting gesture and I can hear them whisper to Alex, asking if he is alright. When Alex tells them that they are fine, they turn around to face me, anger flaring in her perfect aquamarine eyes.

"What do you think you're doing Luis?" I have never had Colomba direct anger like this at me before. I don't understand what's going on. I clear my throat and try to smile at her, even though I know I probably look awkward since I feel very uncomfortable with her anger directed at me.

"C'mon Colomba, it's just Alex. I mean, the guy needs a little motivation to not be such an idiot. We are just helping him a little by doing this, it will make sure he tries harder after this so that he won't have this happen to him again. I guess you could say I'm doing a bit of charity work with him." The crowd around me laughs, but Colomba doesn't even crack a smile.

"Is this because I refused to go on a date with you earlier today?" The entire crowd falls silent at that, worry coming across their face, as if they think I will get angry and do something terrible in response to this. "Are you really taking your anger out on Alex because of that, that's just pathetic Luis. You need to work on your emotional intelligence so that you won't act like this anymore and disgust people further." I hear a few people gasp at her words. Some people look at each other as if silently asking what they think is going to happen. It's almost as if they are afraid that I will do something terrible to Colomba because she said that. Am I really so horrible in this world that they would think I could do something bad to someone as wonderful as Colomba? What have a done in this world? Am I the monster in this school, just like how Alex is in my school?

"Colomba, I-" She holds up her hand, stopping me.

"Don't bother, I don't want to hear anymore from the likes of you. C'mon Alex, you shouldn't stay here around people like him." She holds out her hand to Alex to help him up, which he eagerly accepts, looking at Colomba like she is an angel. The two of them walk out of the crowd and down the hall, leaving me alone in the crowd with an empty water bottle in my hand. The crowd starts to leave, while I stay in place, watching Colomba and Alex as they continue walking down the hallway. One guy from the disappearing crowd comes up to me and gives me a faint, comforting smile.

"Don't worry Luis, Colomba will come around some day and realize you are the most logical choice for her to be with, and she'll realize how illogical it is for her to protect fools like him. She just has a soft heart, but she's a smart girl, she will realize the truth sooner or later." I nod my head at them and try to look like I believe in what they say, but I know that will never happen. In Colomba's eyes I saw hatred. In this new world, Colomba hates me. She hates me because in this world I am the villain. I am the bully that I have always hated. She will never love me, no matter how much everyone else here likes me. In this world, I am a terrible person, and Colomba would never give her heart to someone like me.

I need to get out of here. I don't care if the entire world loves me here, if Colomba hates me then this place isn't worth it.

Rushing through the hallways, I make my way to one of the bathrooms. Checking it quickly to make sure there is nobody inside, I lift up my sweater to look at my shirt underneath where I hide my Crow Medal. My heart stops in my chest, I take off the sweater to look for the medal, but I still can't find it. I search through my pockets, and I even dump out my backpack to look through everything I have, but it's still not there. Panic overwhelms me for a moment, thinking that I somehow lost it, before I realize the blood chilling truth. Just like I had realized moments ago, in this world, I am a terrible person. The Crow Medal only works for those with a good heart. In this world, I don't have a good heart, so I was never given the Medal, I never met Shadow, and I have lived a normal life. Because of this, I know that I can't contact my soldier and leave this world. No matter how much I want to leave, I am trapped in a world I am responsible for creating.

What am I going to do? Am I stuck here for the rest of my life? If I am, I need to find a way to make Colomba remember who I really am. I can't be trapped here if she hates me, I would slowly die living in a world like that.

Chapter Fifteen
Colomba-
Confusion and
Fear

Leaving class, I head straight for my next one which is study hall. Since I am all caught up on my homework and projects, I can just relax today, which is good since I could use some time to just let my mind rest. It has been a long day; I had that big test, I had that weird run in with Luis in the gym, and then I had to deal with Luis picking on Alex again. I swear, does that guy ever show kindness to anyone? I mean, he's nice to me, most of the time, but that's only because he wants me to be his girlfriend. I would rather date a crazy, scary monster than him though. All I can hope is that he will give up on me one day.

Poor Alex. He has to deal with so much because of Luis. Alex gets picked on constantly since he is not very smart, but he still has some good qualities about him that everyone always seems to ignore. He's very strong and is able to help out a lot because of it, and he is also very kind. Sometimes kindness can be hard to find in a world where everyone is always trying to compete to be the smartest. When you aren't very intelligent like Alex, it must feel like the world forgets about you when the world only wants intelligent people.

After what happened with Luis, I got Alex to a part of the hallway where there weren't any people. I was able to comfort him and help him calm down before we both had to get to our next class. The poor guy looked like he was starting to break down in tears. When I was able to get him alone, I was able to dry those tears, but I know he probably still feels terrible. Alex tells me a lot about how he wishes he could be smart like a lot of the other people in this school, but he feels like he can never be good enough. A guy as kind and gentle as him deserves so much better from this world. I help him a lot with homework and tutor him often, but I don't feel like it is enough. He tells me all the time how grateful he is for my help, but I think he is also just grateful to have a friend willing to help him. I think he wants to be more than friends though to be honest. He's not very good at hiding the fact that he has a crush on me. He is a good guy, don't get me wrong, but I would never want to date him. I want a guy who is as smart as I am, someone I can have a real conversation with that I would enjoy. Sadly, Alex can't do that. Honestly, if Luis was an actually nice person, he would pretty much be the perfect guy for me. I don't see him changing any time in the near future though, so I doubt that will ever happen. I will just have to find someone else in the future, for now though I want to just focus on my studies. I can find love after that.

I make it to study hall, and when I tell the teacher that I don't have anything to work on they let me go to the library to get a book to read. The hallways are empty during this time since everyone else is in class, only the janitor robots are around sweeping up anything that they can find, which isn't much since everyone respects the school and they all try not to make a mess. It doesn't take long to get to the library, find the book I want, and then head back out to get back to the classroom. The hall is so quiet that I can hear my footsteps echoing all around me. It is so peaceful in this silence, but that silent peace is broken when I hear another set of footprints echoing along with mine, but they are moving much faster than mine. My heart immediately starts to race as I turn around quickly to see who is running towards me. When I look back at the hallway behind me, I almost roll my eyes in irritation when I see who it is.

"What do you want Luis?" I grumble with annoyance as he slows down to walk by my side. He looks down at me with a hopeful smile and on the inside, I groan a little bit thinking that he is going to ask me out again. He usually asks me out at least once a week, usually wanting me to go to his art shows and such with him. I do love going to art exhibits and stuff like that, but I would rather not go with him. I could think of a thousand things I would rather do than be around him longer than a few minutes.

"There's something that I really want to show

you that I think you will find interesting." He says this almost nervously, almost like Luis has suddenly become shy. Well that's really weird, Luis has never acted shy before, even when asking me out when most people get embarrassed. In his hand is a very large piece of paper, not something uncommon for an artsy guy like Luis to be holding. He has it rolled up like he has a project he is working on. A little bit of curiosity comes over me, but not enough to make me want to spend any more time with him than I already have.

"No Luis, I need to get back to class." I start walking faster to try and show him that I am not interested in talking to him anymore, but he doesn't get the hint. A sudden look of fear comes over him, as if the world will end if I do not see this.

"Colomba, wait, I need to show you this it's very important!" I stop walking and roll my eyes, knowing that he won't stop bugging me until I do this.

"Alright, fine, what is it Luis?" He smiles joyfully at me, as if I am giving him hope just for doing this. What is up with him today? Luis has been acting so strangely today, almost like he's a completely different person. Without saying another word, he pulls out the large piece of paper and unrolls it to show me a beautiful picture sketched with pencil.

The dark grey lines show a young woman sitting on the root of a large tree in the middle of a garden. It kind of looks like the tree in my backyard. The girl has a peaceful expression on her face as she looks at whoever is sketching her.

Flowers are all around the girl, and I can tell that the wind is blowing since her dress is billowing around her ankles and her hair is going out of place, yet she still looks beautiful. As I look closer at the drawing, I realize that the girl looks familiar. Focusing my eyes on her face, I finally recognize that this girl is me. Luis has always been a good artist, but the image in that picture is better than anything I have ever seen him do before.

For some reason though, I can see this simple pencil sketch as a painting with bright, vibrant colors. Within a flash, I see this painting with a blue ribbon on it like what you would see at a county fair. Luis has won many awards for his work, but I have never seen this one before. I know I haven't seen it before, since I have never modeled for any of his work, and I am the one in the picture. I know I haven't seen it, so why does it look so familiar? I look back up at Luis, suddenly feeling a little afraid of him.

"What is this?" I slowly take a few steps away from him. Luis' eyes show concern when he sees me do this.

"Please, don't be afraid Colomba, you recognize this don't you?" I shake my head no, but from the fear I am showing on my face, he can obviously tell that I am lying since hope seems to light up his eyes.

"Yes you do. You let me paint you once so that I could put it in the county fair, and I won." So I was right about the ribbon, that did mean something. "You let me paint you since we are friends. The Crow gave someone power and they changed the world into this. Nobody else remembers the old world except me, but you remember it too, deep down. You know that I am your friend, and all of this is a lie. You have to remember who I am. I can't let myself live without you by my side."

It feels like there's no air left in the world. I think I might pass out. What is going on with my head right now? I know this painting, I know that I have seen it, and I know that what he is saying is the truth, but I can't believe it, I won't.

I turn and walk away from Luis without saying another word, not sure of what I could say anyway. I have no words to describe how I feel right now. Luis is yelling at me to come back, that I have to believe him, but I don't look back, I just keep going. I'm practically running away from him like a cat running away from an angry dog. My breathing sounds like I've been running up a mountain all day and my head is spinning. It feels like ages before I can find a space to relax on my own, a stall in the girl's bathroom. Only when I am there do I stop moving, letting myself take deep breaths to try and get my heart to stop pounding.

Why is this so frightening to me? I mean, it is just a picture, right? I shake my head, knowing that it is not the picture that scares me, but what the picture means. If that picture and what I remembered is real, then what Luis was saying is real, and the world I am currently living in is fake. I don't want to let myself believe that, I can't. I've lived a very good life that I have been very happy with. My whole family is here; my dad, my mom, and Nonna. They are all here for me, I don't want to let that go. The other world he was talking about could be a whole lot worse. I could be unhappy there and be all alone. I know that what he was telling me is probably a lie, but the little glimpse I saw in that other life still stays in my mind. Maybe I should text my mom, she usually knows what to do. She always has the best advice. My mom has had to live with so much; she was always so sick as a kid but was able to make it through all that due to how good modern medicine is. I'll text her as soon as I get back to the study hall room. I just need to feel safe and comforted, and there is nobody on earth who does that better than my mom.

Chapter Sixteen
Luis-
Lost

The sketch I made of Colomba sits rolled up on my desk as the teacher talks about the history of some war, I'm not sure. I can't really focus on them very well when my heart feels like it has been sucked out of my chest. I don't know what to do. At first, I loved this world Demetrius created, but now it feels like I am living in a nightmare. Everyone seems to love me here, but not the most important person. I'm not even the Crow in this world, and I can't find Demetrius, so how can I fix this? I might be stuck in this horrible world forever. I tried getting Colomba to remember with this picture, and it seemed to work, but she practically ran away from me. Why did she do that? I mean, I could see it in her eyes that she recognized it. She looked a little frightened by it, probably because she started remembering everything and it freaked her out a bit. I would be creeped out too if I started remembering a life I didn't know I had seconds before. Or was she scared of me in that moment? I mean, I guess I was being a little pushy with trying to have her remember me, but I was doing it for good reasons. I don't want to scare her, but she needs to remember who we are to each other, best friends. Even though, in this world, I am surrounded by people who consider themselves to be my friends, she feels like the only friend who truly matters, and I've lost her.

As I sit at my desk, moping, a sound coming from outside that makes the dark thoughts disappear. Looking outside, it looks like a storm is approaching. Wind is blowing forcefully through the trees, sending leaves flying through the air like frightened birds. The howling of the wind seems to grow louder and louder, like someone screaming from a distance coming closer to us. It becomes so loud that the teacher stops talking and the other students start to look outside as well. I suddenly notice something strange, and it makes the hairs on the back of my neck stand up straight. This isn't a storm, there isn't a dark cloud in the sky, something else is causing this.

The others can tell that something is weird too, and two of the other students stand up to look out the window. One of them lets out a shout in shock while the other one looks paralyzed with fear while they point up at something off to the side of the building, out of view for the rest of us. Everyone instantly runs towards the windows to see what is going on, and we look off to the other side of the building to see something that fills me with terror as well as a bit of hope. A massive machine, about the size of a bus, is flying in front of the school. The wind seems to be coming from that thing since it is using a giant fan on the bottom of it to keep it up in the air. Some students are already leaving the school through the front doors to see what this thing is, and I follow right after them because my nightmare might finally be able to end.

Sprinting down the hall with the other curious students following me, I am almost crying with relief as hope grows stronger in me. I might finally have someone who can get this world back to the way it was, because standing on top of that machine was Demetrius, the genius who caused all this. Maybe I can convince him to get things back to the way they were. Maybe I can finally go home. Maybe I can finally have Colomba in my life again. I know that I haven't even been here a full day, but it feels like an eternity has passed since I arrived. I don't care if I get made fun of and beaten down in my old world, at least there I have the one light in my life that truly matters, Colomba. I practically burst through the front doors of the school, ready to talk to the monster I have created. No matter what happens, I need to talk to him.

Chapter Seventeen
Colomba-
The Genius

I am swallowed within the massive crowd of students rushing through the front doors, trying to see what on earth this strange thing is flying above the school. Thankfully, I am near the front of the crowd, so I am one of the first there. As soon as I burst through the front doors, the wind whips my hair over my face, and I have to brush it away to get a good look at this strange thing. This machine is massive, almost the length of two buses on all sides. Everyone around me is so stunned by what we are seeing that nobody speaks or even makes a sound as we all look up at this mechanical monstrosity.

It is flying about thirty feet in the air thanks to a massive fan that lets it stay above the ground, but creates a wind so strong that I have to fight with my hair to be able to see. The thing is made of a silver metal that shines so brilliantly in the dim winter sunlight that I am almost blinded looking up at it. With the fan that lets it fly spinning so fast that it doesn't make a sound, it is a silent menace that hangs above all of us. The crowd below it just looks at each other, wondering what will happen. After a moment, the shock seems to wear off, and people start talking, asking each other if they know what is going on, but nobody seems to know anything about it.

When it seems like everyone's curiosity has become too much for us to handle, I notice something move at the top of the machine. It is something small considering how big this machine is, yet it seems that everyone else has noticed it too since the crowd has fallen silent again as we wait to see if it will appear again. After a minute, I start to think that I may have imagined it all, until the figure of a person appears standing on top of the machine. I have to squint my eyes to be able to see them clearly, but when I do, my mouth falls open in shock. It's Demetrius, one of the smartest kids in the entire school. What on earth is he doing up there? Is this another one of his mechanical marvels that he wanted to show off? All the other students seem to think so too, since they all smile and wave up at Demetrius, yelling to him that his machine is amazing and that this is a really cool surprise. Demetrius doesn't seem to hear or care about what they say since he screams down to everyone with a voice full of rage.

"I am Demetrius, and I am the smartest being in this world! With my intelligence I can do far more than any other being on this planet can! I have come to rule over you to create a better world! Now who shall follow me!?" Everyone in the crowd looks away from him to look at each other with the same confused expression. I raise my hand to get this his attention on me.

"You're the smartest by whose standards?!" Demetrius suddenly appears very shocked by my words, as if he can't believe I just said that. A guy beside me decides to continue my argument.

"She's right, who can really say who is the smartest considering intelligence is very difficult to measure?!" A girl somewhere in the crowd joins in as well.

"Yes, and what kind of intelligence are we speaking of; are we talking about book smarts, musical intelligence, or something else?! What are we talking about here?!" I decide to join back in with the argument.

"Yes, and if you are the smartest in only one form of intelligence, that doesn't really make a good leader, especially the leader of the entire world! I mean the world is too large of a place for one person to rule alone! An entire council of people would be needed for something like that!" A few other people start to chime in to argue against Demetrius and discuss what would be needed for someone to "rule the world". While they are all distracted by this, I slip out of the crowd and head into the girl's bathroom to have a little privacy. I have something that I need to do. As soon as I am sure that I am alone, I place my hand on top of the Dove Pin and say the magic words. The entire room is filled with a blinding light, but only for a second. When it is gone, so am I, and in my place is Silver Dove. I rush out of the room, ready to take on this fight. A dark part of my mind can't help but wonder though, is this the guy that Luis was trying to tell me is the one who changed the world into what I remember it as?

I don't have time to let these thoughts get to me though, there's a guy causing issues in this school, and I need to go kick his butt. I can't wait until this fight is done; my mom is going to love hearing about this. I've never fought someone with super powers before, so this should be really cool, I know Mom will think so too. I kick off the ground and soar through the halls, ready to take on my newest enemy. This is going to be awesome!

Chapter Eighteen
Luis-
The Other Crow

All around me, people are making logical arguments about what is needed for a person to rule the world while Demetrius is standing on top of his machine, looking down at everyone with complete shock. Honestly, I can't believe what I'm hearing either. He said that he's going to take over the world and instead of freaking out, everyone is just discussing it calmly like they are sitting at the dinner table talking with their family about what they did that day. How is everyone so calm about this?! This is nuts!

I wave my hands above my head to try and get Demetrius' attention, hoping and praying that he will notice me so that I can try to talk with him and get the world changed to the way it was. He doesn't even look at me though, he is too busy glaring at the people having the discussion about being the ruler of the world. It looks like Demetrius is about to start yelling at these people when a strange sound, almost like the sound of something flying quickly through the air, suddenly makes everyone fall silent and start looking around. It only takes a few seconds before someone gives out a shout of joy and points over the school. I follow their gaze to see a large creature with massive wings flying over the school. Great, Silver Dove is here, she can defeat this guy and then life can go back to normal. This is probably the only time I've ever been happy to see Silver Dove coming to save the day.

The entire crowd breaks out into cheers, and a few start chanting something that makes me look back at the winged person above the school, realizing I made a mistake. That isn't Silver Dove coming to save the day. It is the person everyone is now chanting their name, that is this world's version of the Crow. The Crow stops in front of Demetrius, staring at him with confidence clearly being shown from behind that mask. Demetrius' face clearly shows his shock since he can tell the person in front of him isn't me. I look at the Crow of this world carefully. This guy has paler skin than me, yet also has a tan, showing that he spends a lot of time outside. He is also really muscular, like he does a lot of sports. When I recognize the light brown hair of this guy, it feels like someone has punched me in the gut. I start breathing heavily, trying to fill my empty lungs, trying to feel alive even though the realization makes me feel like I am dead. The Crow of this world… it's Alex.

How on earth could Alex be the Crow here?! He's a horrible person! The Medal only works for someone with a good heart, how could he… oh wait, in this world he does have a good heart. In this world he is the bullied kid with no friends and

Colomba has to protect him. He has a good heart; while I am the popular kid with everyone as my friend, but Colomba doesn't want anything to do with me, and I have a dark heart. I've always wanted to be able to switch places with Alex, to be the one that doesn't get hurt and has a ton of friends. Well now I have it, and I hate it. Tears start to sting in my eyes as the crowd grows silent so that Alex as the Crow can speak to Demetrius.

"Demetrius, what are you doing? Why are you talking about taking over the world? You've never acted like this before." Alex's voice sounds confident as the Crow, much different than the quiet, frightened voice he had when I was dumping the water on him earlier today. Even though his voice is confident and loud enough for the crowd to hear him, he does not sound intimidating like when I am the Crow. His voice is gentle yet strong, like a father scolding a small child.

It only takes a minute for Demetrius to get over his shock at seeing a different Crow. Honestly, with how smart I made him, he has probably already figured out why Alex and I switched places. Demetrius chuckles at him, even from all the way down here, I can see a little bit of crazy in Demetrius' eyes as he does this. The Crow even backs up a little when seeing that, I don't blame him, I'm pretty far away and I still want to run away too.

Another cheer goes out in the crowd, and I look to where some people are pointing to see another figure flying through the air towards us. I let out a sigh of relief as everyone else starts screaming

Silver Dove's name. She still looks the same as the old world, so she is probably the same person, she will know how to handle this, she always seems to know.

Her snowy white wings stop her right in front of the machine so that she is flying right next to the Crow. He smiles at her sappily, like he is a puppy looking at its master, while Silver Dove just greets him with a head nod before she turns to look at Demetrius. I have a feeling that things are about to go nuts. Everyone else seems to feel this too, since the crowd starts to run back into the school for shelter, but I stay where I am. I need to be a part of this. I need to help where I can to make sure that we all get back home. I need to end this. I need to see my Colomba again, and I will risk everything to stay here to make sure that happens.

Chapter Nineteen
Colomba-
Fighting Fire

The Crow and my wings seem to be the only sound at the moment as I see everyone go back into the school from the corner of my eye. Thank goodness everyone has the common sense to get away from all this, if anything goes wrong with Demetrius I don't know if I could protect everyone. This is kind of a new situation for me to deal with. I've never dealt with someone creating a giant mechanical thing trying to take over the world, I feel like a comic book hero right now. It's kinda cool, and also really scary… I guess more scary than cool. I might die today… oh gosh. Now all the coolness of this moment is gone, now I'm just scared out of my mind. I try to not let that show though as I glare at Demetrius from behind my mask.

"What are you doing Demetrius? Why are you talking about taking over the world like some weird movie villain?" Demetrius just glares back at me, looking at me like I'm a little kid messing up his stuff.

"I should have known that you would still exist in this world." I look over to the Crow, who just shrugs at me, just as confused as I am.

"What do you mean by this wor-?" I stop right in the middle of the word as a sudden sinking feeling hits me right in the gut. Another world? Was Luis telling me the truth earlier? Is there another world that we are all from that only a few people truly remember? I look at Demetrius with horror on my face. "They were right, you were the one who changed the world into what it is now."

The Crow stares at me as if I have gone crazy. I can't blame him though, if I didn't know what was going on, and I heard someone say that, I would think they were nuts too. I turn to the Crow, ready to sound like a complete nutcase so I can explain this to him.

"Someone told me earlier today that someone was given powers by the Crow in another world, and that person changed the world into what it is now. I started remembering parts of that world, so I now know that they were telling the truth, and I believe we are looking at the person who changed everything." Demetrius just chuckles at me as if I have just figured out a horrible secret. Crow looks at him like he is looking at a monster, and I can't help but agree.

"Why would you do this Demetrius? Everyone loves you, why would you want to make people afraid of you like this?" Demetrius' smile immediately fades as rage begins to burn in his eyes.

"Nobody likes me in the other world, but now I

am the smartest being on Earth, so I can take over this world and make sure that it runs the way it should be." I just look at him, completely shocked.

"Just because things are bad for some people, doesn't mean that you change everything. This isn't real, it's just something that you created. If you are the "smartest being on Earth" as you put it, then you should know that. Whatever your problems are in that world, I will help you get through it. I promise." Demetrius stares at me as if he can't believe what I am saying, but someone else seems to agree with me too.

"She's right!!" I turn around, surprised by who I see speaking up against this dangerous weirdo. Luis walks up to stand beneath me, looking up at this guy bravely, like he has nothing to fear at all. "You can't live in a world that you know isn't real Demetrius! You made this new world, but it isn't real! You thought this world wouldn't have any problems, but the same problems are still here that you were dealing with back home! People are still hurting each other; the only difference is who is getting hurt! You didn't get rid of the problem you just made it a little different! You said that people like me would be happy here, but I'm not! I've lost the most important thing in my life here! You stole them from me!"

Demetrius actually pauses, looking down at Luis as if he has been hurt by what Luis is saying. Are he and Luis good friends in this other world they remember? Is that why Demetrius is actually listening to him and feeling bad about what he has said? As I look at Luis with shock, I feel a bit impressed by how brave he is being, I can only manage to ask one simple question.

"Why are you helping me, Luis?" He finally turns his eyes away from Demetrius to look at me, his eyes full of pain and fear.

"Because I know that something is wrong here too. I remember what the other world was like. I know that I am supposed to be friends with Colomba, and not be this horrible person that I am here. We are supposed to be best friends, and I want to be back in that world." My heart feels like it is about to burst with the happiness I have. A sudden image of Luis, but with long hair hanging in his face fills my mind. That image of him is smiling shyly at me as we chat in the cafeteria like the best of friends. With that image in my mind, I know now that he has been telling me the truth the whole time. He is my friend, and more than anything I want that friend in my life again.

I turn my attention away from him to look at Demetrius, who is still staring down at Luis with absolute shock on his face, almost as if he feels betrayed by Luis saying that. Why would he feel betrayed by Luis though? That doesn't make sense. I break him out of that shock though with one simple question.

"So Demetrius, are you going to listen to everyone here and get things back to normal, or will we have to settle things another way?" I pull out my sword to show him exactly what I mean by "another way". Demetrius tears his eyes away from Luis to glare at me with enough hatred to make me shiver a little. I don't think I've ever seen anyone look at me like this, except maybe the time I was little and I spilled a soda on a guy near me and my mom had to stop him from yelling at me. That was really scary. Yeah, probably shouldn't be thinking about that right now, something much scarier is happening. Demetrius is practically shaking in his rage, I can hear him breathing deeply, like he is about to explode. Suddenly, he points towards me and screams.

"Fire." Before I can react, from the corner of my eye I see a laser shoot in a blast of red light right at me and I fly backwards and fall towards the ground, my wings getting covered in mud and fallen winter leaves. I shake my wings to try and get some of that off of me as I pick myself off the ground. The Crow flies next to me, worry painted all over his face.

"Are you alright Silver Dove?" he asks, looking me over to see if he can find any injuries. I am lucky that I have a partner like him. It wasn't long after I got my powers that I found out that Alex was the one behind the Crow mask. We have been working together ever since. He is everything you could want in a crime fighting partner; he is loyal, works hard, and is always willing to help me in a fight and is always looking out for me. I am lucky to have him. I chuckle at his question.

"Don't worry Alex, I can't get hurt remember?" I say this to make him feel better, but I don't tell him that even though I can't hurt, I can still feel pain, and I feel like I have just been hit by a truck. Looking back up at the machine, I notice something that sends a chill down my spine. A nozzle, like what firetrucks use to spray water from, is sticking out of the giant machine, but instead of water dripping out of it, I see a little bit of flame starting to form. Without thinking, I grab Alex and fly into the air just as a giant cloud of fire sprays from the machine right where we were only seconds before. The smell of burnt grass makes my nose tingle, and I want to sneeze, but I hold it in, not wanting to distract myself for even a moment. A maniac willing to try to fry us is not someone you want to be distracted around. Alex looks at the charred ground beneath us in absolute horror before he turns to Demetrius with fury burning in his eyes.

"What is wrong with you?! You could have killed us!!" Demetrius chuckles at him, as if the answer is obvious.

"That's the plan! Whoever gets in my way will be eliminated! They are standing in the way of progress and will be punished!" My heart stops when I hear a small voice coming from the ground below us, and I look down to see that Luis is still standing in front of the machine like a complete lunatic.

"Stop this Demetrius!! This isn't what you wanted, is it?!" Luis screams at Demetrius, and even though I know Demetrius can hear him, I can tell that he is trying to not look at Luis. He doesn't want to even think about the questions Luis is asking.

Closing my wings, I start falling towards the ground like a missle. I need to get Luis out of here, I need to protect him. When I am only a few feet from the ground, I open my wings back out again, catching myself in the air so that I am soaring only three feet off the ground. I am practically racing against death as I feel some more of the machine's lasers firing at me. Since I am moving so fast though, they are hitting behind me, just barely missing my feet. I can feel the heat from the lasers cooking my toes. As I get closer to Luis who is looking at the chaos around him in pure terror, I open my arms wide like I am trying to give him a big hug. Instead of hugging him though, when I reach him, I wrap my arms around him and carry him into the air, trying to put as much distance as possible between us and the machine. The farther he is from all this, the safer he will be. As soon as I have Luis in my grasp, Demetrius' machine focuses its attention on Alex.

Weird, why did it suddenly change targets as soon as I picked up Luis? Wait, I can't let myself get distracted by that, I need to act, and I need to do it now. I only start slowing down when I am two blocks away from the school, a distance that I am sure will keep Luis safe. Setting him down gently, I look him over to make sure that he wasn't hurt during all of that. I don't see any injuries, but in his eyes I can tell that, on the inside, he is pretty messed up. In those dark eyes I see misery and guilt. Why does he feel guilty? Is it because he is a different person in the other world, and feels bad about the kind of person he is in this world? I could understand that, but why would he be feeling that now while all of this is going on? I think that there would be a better time to think about all that when there isn't a crazy guy shooting lasers at everyone.

"Wait here, when it all quiets down it should be safe for you to come back, don't move until that happens." I am about to start flying off to rejoin the fight when Luis says something that frightens me, stopping me dead in my tracks.

"I can help, let me come back with you."

"No!!!" I scream at him in my fear. He actually backs up a bit in surprise at my reaction. I take in a deep breath before I speak again, in a much calmer tone. "No Luis, this is not a fight you can win. You do not have any powers like me, you cannot defend yourself against something like that machine. Stay here where you are safe, let the Crow and I handle it. We will find a way to solve this." I start flying back to the fight, and I hear Luis yelling behind me, but I don't let myself listen. I have a fight to win, and I can't let his words get in my way.

It only takes a few seconds for me to fly the two blocks back to the school to see that Alex is still fighting Demetrius' mechanical monster. Alex has created an army of his shadow tigers, who are now leaping at the machine' trying to get on top of it to get at Demetrius. None of his creatures makes it to the top though; lasers are firing from all sides of this crazy thing, destroying his creatures if they get too close. I can't just fly up to try and get Demetrius, I'll just get shot down like Alex's shadow tigers before I can ever reach him. I need to be more clever about this. The machine seems to be flying because of the giant fan on the bottom of this thing; if I mess with that then it should fall to the ground and then we can take care of things from there.

Flying low to the ground, I swerve past Alex's

shadow tigers until I am right underneath the machine. With nothing but a prayer that this will work, I throw my sword into the fan keeping the machine in the air. An ear-splitting crunch and grinding sound comes from the machine as soon as my sword hits it. The fan stops, and I see my sword sticking out of what looks like an engine. With the fan stopped, the machine immediately begins to drop, and I fly out of the way to avoid getting hit, but there is no point. As soon as it started to fall, a loud beeping, like a warning siren, goes off in the machine and four metal legs spring out from the sides of the machine and catch the machine before it was able to drop five feet. I release a groan of annoyance as the machine starts to walk around in front of the school like a demented giant robot spider.

"Why did he have to make it difficult? Why can't this just be easy?" Alex shows his frustration as he orders his shadow tigers to start climbing the new legs of this creature to try and make it to the top. The dark creatures swarm over the monster, trying desperately to destroy it, but the lasers keep firing at them, making the tigers disappear into the nothingness they truly are. Is this thing unstoppable or what?

Lifting up my hand, I focus on my sword still trapped in the mechanisms of the machine. A terrible metallic ripping sound screeches through the air as my sword pries itself out of the creation and flies right back into my hand. I'm definitely going to need this sword; seems I have a difficult job on my hands. Flying straight at one of the legs, I swing the sword right at it, hoping to snap it to pieces so the thing can fall and Alex can bury this thing under a pile of his shadow tigers, but I am not so lucky. I am not sure what this thing is made of, but my sword doesn't even scratch this thing. I have super strength and a magic sword; how did that not do anything?!!! I hack and slash at this thing, but nothing happens, I am trying to win a losing battle. Okay I need to think of something else. I can't just try and fly up at Demetrius on top since his machine will just shoot lasers at me again and send me back to the ground, just like it's currently doing with Alex's shadow tigers. There must be some way to break through his defense.

My heart stops as I hear a voice in the distance yelling out to the three of us fighting. My head snaps to the side to see Luis running right towards us, he must have run the distance I flew to get him away from the fight. Why did he come back?!! Is he nuts?!!! He is waving his arms frantically, like he is trying to get our attention. Well, I guess his plan worked, all of my attention is now all on him.

"Luis!! Are you crazy?!! Get out of here!!! You're going to get yourself killed!!!" I know that Luis can hear me, but he doesn't pay any attention to what I'm saying. All his attention is on Demetrius at the top of the machine. I can hear Luis screaming Demetrius' name, but I don't think Demetrius can hear him, he is looking down at Alex who is trying to create more of his tigers as fast as he can while Demetrius' machine is destroying them as fast as he can make them. As I watch them, the lasers are moving closer and closer to Alex, obviously trying to hit Alex. Alex is too busy trying to create his army though, and he does not notice this.

Luis must have noticed this before me, since he is running towards Alex before I can even move. I start flapping my wings even though I know it is already too late. Luis makes it to Alex first, stopping to stand right in front of Alex with his arms spread out wide as if he is trying to protect him. The instant he does this, the chaos around us immediately stops, and from the corner of my eye I can see that the machine is no longer firing anything at Alex, as if Demetrius is afraid of hitting Luis. I notice this when I am only a few yards from reaching them, only seconds pass before I make it to Luis, snatching him up in my arms again so that he is out of the way. Once I have him in my arms again, I can hear the machine firing again, but Alex now has the time to get out of the way and create a couple more tigers to help protect himself, so with him safe, I can focus on the lunatic I am currently carrying.

"Luis, I swear, you have to be the craziest idiot I have ever met in my whole life, but I'm going to need you!" Luis stares at me with wide eyed shock, but stays silent so that I can explain. "You and Demetrius must have been friends in the old world so he didn't want to hurt you, if I can get you on top you might be able to talk him out of doing this. You okay with that?!"

Luis' shock disappears to be replaced by pure determination, he gives me a simple nod and I know what to do. Flying straight into the air, I get above the machine, behind Demetrius so he can't quite see us yet. I swoop down a bit and drop Luis down on top of the machine before letting myself down as well to finally face the creator of this monster.

"Demetrius, stop this!" Demetrius turns around in terror, realizing that he is no longer alone up here. With him distracted, Alex's tigers manage to climb up as well and start encircling all of us, keeping their glowing red eyes on Demetrius. Behind him, Alex flies up and watches what is happening, but not attacking yet when he sees what we are doing. "This has to end! Look at what you have done!!" Luis points towards the front courtyard of the school. Demetrius follows his gesture to see that the once well-maintained courtyard is now completely destroyed, smoking a little from the burnt grass from his lasers. In the windows I can see the other students looking outside absolutely terrified and some of them sobbing as they watch what is going on. Demetrius looks shocked by this, as if he hadn't realized what he was doing only moments ago. Luis speaks to him again, in a much gentler tone this time.

"I know that this isn't what you wanted Demetrius. You told me that you wanted to change the world. For a person like you, you would have changed it to what you thought would make it better, some things have changed, but the people are still just like they were in the old world. People still get made fun of here, people still get hurt. The only difference is who is getting hurt. It may not be you here, but it is so many others Demetrius." He pauses for a moment, and I see tears welling up in Luis' eyes before he speaks again. "I have become a horrible person here. I was made fun of all the time in the old world, I was miserable and in pain, but now I hurt others. I give the pain that I wouldn't wish on anyone." Luis chokes back his words before his anger returns to him. "None of this is real! This is a world you made up! For someone as smart as you, you should realize this! Change it back to the way it was!" Demetrius appears to be thinking about Luis has said, but isn't fully convinced yet. I guess it's my turn to try and get him to stop this.

"Demetrius, I'm guessing you changed this world because you felt like things weren't right over there? That you were getting hurt there? Things aren't any different here though; people are still in pain and miserable. The only thing that's probably different is who feels this pain and why." Luis nods his head at that, as if I am right in my guess.

"She's right. You got the power to do all this from the Crow in our world, he gave you these powers because people hurt you since you were so much smarter than them. So you changed the world to be like this, where all anyone cares about is how smart you are." I feel my eyes grow wide behind my mask. That's what all this is about?! Demetrius was upset since he got made fun of for being smart?! What kind of world is this where you get made fun of for being smart and the Crow will give you powers to do something like this?! How stupid is the Crow in that world that he would give powers away like that?! I can't think of stuff like this; for right now I have to return to the world we are talking about.

"Demetrius, being smart isn't something you should get teased for, and I am sorry that you have to go through with that, but being smart is something you should be praised for. Intelligent people are the ones who really create the world, not the strong, and not the ones causing wars. The smart ones create all the things we need in life and make everything more comfortable for everyone. If someone makes fun of you or tries to take advantage of you because of how smart you are, then that just shows how stupid they are. They know that you have a better chance at succeeding in life because you are smarter than them, and they hate you for that, but that's okay. You can be happy in that world, if you let yourself be. You are smart enough to realize that you are in charge of your own happiness. If someone is trying to bring you down you should be smart enough to realize that you have options on how to deal with that, you choose your destiny. Now stop trying to control the destiny of others, and let us all return home to the real world."

Silence falls over the four of us; Demetrius lowers his head as he thinks about what we have said, Luis and I stand in front of him waiting to see what happens, and Alex is still flying behind Demetrius, ready and waiting for something to happen so that he can let his tigers pounce on Demetrius. After a tense minute of waiting, Demetrius finally looks back up at Luis and I.

"I will program the machine to reverse everything, it will just take me a minute, alright?" He doesn't even wait for a reply, he just opens up a metal panel in his machine to reveal countless wires and such that he starts messing with. He probably wants to be alone to focus on that, so instead I turn to Luis.

"Thank you Luis for your help. I wouldn't have been able to even make it up here to talk with him if I didn't have you." Luis appears uncomfortable talking to me, I wonder why. He clears his throat awkwardly before he speaks to me.

"Yeah of course… happy to help." Luis turns away from me, as if he is eager to get away from me. Weird. Oh well, I have someone else I need to speak to. Walking over to the edge of the machine, I look at Alex who lowers himself so that he is flying right in front of me. The two of us smile at each other with a bit of sadness hidden behind it. We both know what could happen, we may not be the Crow and Silver Dove in that world, we may be completely different there, this may be our last time speaking to each other as friends. We may not even know each other in this other world, we need to say goodbye while we can. I manage to end the silence even though I feel as if I may break down crying any second.

"Alex, whatever happens, I hope that we can still be the best of friends in this other world. I hope I can still remember all of our adventures together…" I pause as I feel a sadness come over my heart when the reality hits me that I may not even remember him in a moment. I look up at him, trying to hold back the tears as I give him a gentle smile. "If we all remember this, please come find me there." Alex looks into my gaze with a pitiful look in his eyes behind that dark mask. He trembles a little as if he is terrified of what is about to happen.

"Colomba, if things don't turn out, and things are different for us on the other side, I just want you to know that… that I- uhh" I smile up at Alex, trying to encourage him to be brave and to tell me what he wants to say so badly. He looks down at my smiling face, and gives me an uncomfortable smile, a smile full of fear about what he is going to say. "I love you." I suddenly feel as if my heart is falling deep into my chest. "I've loved you since the moment I first saw you in gym class. You were just so kind, and gentle, and beautiful. You are what I always dreamed of finding in life. No matter what world we end up in I will always love you, and- I hope- you can love me too."

When those words leave his lips, the world around me begins to fade, but I am not afraid. I want to say something back to him, but I am wrapped in darkness as this world disappears, leaving me in nothingness. I am going back to the real world, and all I can hope is that I will see my good friend on the other side.

Chapter Twenty
Lius-
Back Home

Opening my eyes, I am greeted to the most beautiful sight I could ever see. I am in the gym, the gym of the real world, not the one Demetrius created, and I am in my costume as the Crow while laying on the ground beneath me is Colomba. The real one, the one I have been friends with for years now, the most amazing girl in the world. We are both on the ground, with me on top of her like I was trying to protect her from something. It only takes me a moment to realize that when Demetrius gave up his powers and got his machine to switch back to our regular world, we were taken back to the exact moment before he turned on his machine and created that world. Colomba has opened her eyes underneath me, and seems to have figured out the same thing as me, since she looks so happy and relieved when she sees the gym looking normal again. Her happy expression disappears though when she looks up at me, that happy smile turns into an uncomfortable grimace instantly.

"Oh sorry." I say awkwardly as I pick myself up and then hold out my hand to help her up. Surprisingly, she accepts my hand and I lift her up easily. Turning around, I see Demetrius standing in the center of the gym where his machine had been earlier today when I first walked in here, now he stands alone, staring at the two of us with discomfort.

"I'm sorry for everything guys. Thankfully with how I built the machine, just in case, if I did make everything back to normal, barely anybody would be able to remember the world I created. You two will remember it since you were so close to the machine when it went off, but nobody else will, so you might not want to talk to people about this or they might think you are crazy. Hopefully, I can turn things around for myself. I kinda have a second chance to do that now. I'll see you guys later."

Demetrius walks out of the gym without another word, leaving Colomba and I alone in a very uncomfortable silence. The two of us just look at each other for a moment, unclear about what we should say or do. I clear my throat softly, breaking the tense silence between us.

"I guess I should go too. Goodbye Colomba." I turn and start walking to the door when I hear her finally speak behind me.

"Crow please, we have to talk about all of this. About what just happened. It has to end before things get even worse." I lower my face away from her gaze.

"Yes, I know, and I will stop this." I hear her take in a soft breath of surprise, and I look back up to see her face shining with happy disbelief.

"Do you mean that? Are you done transforming people like this?" I smile softly at her, trying to feel a bit better even though I am pretty much accepting defeat. I have been defeated after almost three years of fighting against Silver Dove.

"Yes, it is all over now. I have tried and failed with this plan far too many times, it is time to give up on it. I have hurt far too many innocent people with this, especially you. I never wanted to hurt you. You are one of the kindest people I have in my life. I would lose everything if I knew I had hurt you. I would die internally. So if you want me to stop this, then I will. There's no point in going on with this plan if I know you are willing to risk everything to try and talk to me alone just to tell me to stop this." I sigh softly, feeling more guilt than I have ever felt in my life. "You deserve better than this, you deserve better than the person I am right now." I look into her perfect aquamarine eyes, and I see everything I need in life. "But I will be better so that I can be worthy of you one day, I promise."

Colomba smiles at me softly, with a bit of pity in her eyes. I turn away from her, not wanting to see the pity in her gaze. I never want her to pity me, but I guess, to her, I am quite the pitiful creature. In my eyes, I'm pretty pitiful too. I am the kid that always gets messed with, I don't really have anything that I can show off about in my life, and even though I have superpowers I can't defeat one person to win a war against this school. Everyone who has ever picked on me is right; I am pathetic, I am a loser, and I don't know if I will ever be worthy of being more than friends with Colomba. She always tries to build me up, encourages me to come out of my shell and see more of the world and myself that I never thought I would see, but in the end, I will always be the same pitiful creature that will always get brought down again.

I smile weakly at her before I walk away. I don't want to leave her, but I know I have to. I can hear her call my name behind me, but I don't turn around, I can't. I know if I do that now then I will stay with her. My footsteps echo in the silent gym, and I can tell that Colomba is standing still and watching me leave since I don't hear any other footsteps except mine. I make it to the door and walk outside into the hallway, instantly transforming back into my regular self as soon as the door is closed. Nobody else is in the hallway right now since class just started a little bit ago. Behind me, in the gym, I can hear footsteps rushing towards me, and I instantly know that Colomba is running towards the door so that she can find me and see who I really am. I sprint down the hallway and into a bathroom right as soon as she makes it out the door and looks around herself, searching for whoever could be the Crow. She does not see me peeking out from behind the bathroom door, but I watch her as she starts to walk down the hallway with disappointment in her eyes as she heads back to her class.

I'm sorry Colomba, but I can't tell you who I really am, not yet at least. That day will come, but we both have to be patient for that day to arrive. For now though, as soon as she is out of sight, I leave the bathroom and head to my next class. I need to just get through this day, and then I'm sure things will be better in the morning because there is an idea stirring in my mind and I'm sure that everything will turn out alright very soon.

Chapter Twenty- One
Colomba-
I Am Home

All around me, people are chatting and having a good time, obviously not knowing what happened earlier today with Demetrius. I feel a bit lonely knowing that I am possibly one of the only people in this school who remembers. The only other people I know who would remember is the Crow and Demetrius, I can only guess if anybody else remembers.

It is now the end of the school day and the crowd I am following is heading towards the front doors, ready to head home for the day. I follow the crowd, but I don't really join in their excitement. I look around the crowd, but nobody else seems to be acting differently, like they had been living completely different lives only an hour or so before now.

As I walk out the front doors, I see several people hanging around Alex's fancy sports car as Alex himself chats with them. I can tell from how he is smiling that he is showing off like usual. He always has a particularly smug grin when he is showing off. He scans the crowd and notices me; from the way he is looking at me so normally, I can tell that he does not remember what happened in the other world. He does not remember confessing his love to me. My heart aches a bit at that thought, why do I feel this way? I don't like Alex at all really, so why do I feel bad that he doesn't remember that?

I suppose it all just makes me wonder about how Alex really feels in this real world. He has been chasing after me since freshman year three years ago; does he still hold on to me because he loves me like his other self said, or does he just want me because he thinks I am pretty? I must have been looking at Alex a little too long though since he gives me one of his flirty little smiles and winks at me. I turn away from him and keep walking to the bus. I'm not going to let him start thinking I'm interested in him, especially after how he acted the other day with Luis. Luis' face is still pretty bruised, why Alex thinks he can act all flirty with me now is beyond me.

As I make my way through the crowd to get to my bus, I bump into someone familiar that I was hoping I wouldn't see for at least another day or so, Demetrius. The second he sees who he bumped into, he looks down at his feet, completely embarrassed. I swallow back my discomfort before I speak to him.

"I'm sorry about that Demetrius." I'm afraid that he is going to try and explain himself for what he did today since he knows I am one of the only people who will remember what he did, but he doesn't. Instead, he says something that turns my blood into ice.

"I'm sorry too, Silver Dove." My heart stops, but Demetrius doesn't even stop to explain how he knows who I really am, he just gives me a faint smile before he starts walking towards his bus, leaving me behind. Was he able to figure it out since the Crow gave him the power of being the most intelligent being on earth? That would make sense, but I am still terrified about him knowing that I'm Silver Dove. As I watch him walk away from me though, I have a feeling that I don't need to worry about him. He will keep my secret, probably because he feels like he owes me that since I helped him get himself out of his fantasy land and back into reality. He has no reason to hate me. I just hope that everything will be alright for him in the end, and he won't feel all this pain anymore. He needs some peace in his life.

The bus ride home is uneventful, and I make it back to my house without any issues. I told Nonna about everything that happened today, and she was very interested in the world he created. She seemed to enjoy the thought of a world where intelligence means everything, I suppose it was a very nice world to live in, but it isn't real, so I guess it's best not to think about it. Now I am lying in my bed, ready to put this crazy day behind me and move on with my life. After all the bad stuff that has been going on recently, I could use some peace. If the Crow keeps his word and stops doing all this terrible stuff, then I might get my wish. I shouldn't trust the Crow to keep his word though, he isn't really the most trustworthy person. He will probably transform another person in a month or two, I wouldn't be surprised at least. I feel my body start growing heavier as I am falling asleep, and I am almost in a dream until my body jerks awake as one thought passes through my mind.

A sudden feeling of horror comes over me and I stop breathing as I realize something truly horrible. Back in that world, my mom was still alive. My heart feels like it is crumbling in my chest at that thought. In the world that the Crow's little minion created, since there were so many crazy smart people in that world, medicine was better there, so my mom was able to survive her illness and I was able to have a life with her. In my mind I can see memories I have of her throughout my life, they are all beautiful memories. We are doing fun things together; going on vacations with the family, going to county fairs, she taught me so much, and she helped me with every problem I had. As I think of all the wonderful times in a life I never really lived, they quickly start fading in my mind as the effects of Demetrius' machine start to disappear. I feel them slipping away as I try to hold on to at least one of them. Please let me just keep one memory of my mother with me to help me cope with her not being with me anymore!

I beg this in my mind, but of course it doesn't do anything. The power of the Crow's spell with his minion is fading, and everything involved in that curse is being taken away, even the memories of a life I could have lived. The memories of a life I always dreamed of having are slipping away and I can't do anything to stop it.

I didn't know it at the time, but by choosing to return to this world, my mom is dead again. Does that mean I killed my mother? Tears are now flowing down my face as I sob into my pillow. Why?! Why is this happening?! It's not my fault! I didn't kill her! That world wasn't real. It was just a fantasy world created by one of the Crow's little minions, nothing more, but that doesn't mean that the thought of losing my mother again doesn't hurt.

It feels like my sobbing goes on forever as one thought seems to circle through my mind. I regret saving the day. I regret leaving the world that the Crow's minion created. In that world I was happy, my family was complete, and the world seemed to be a better place. Now I just have a hollow feeling in my chest that I don't know if it can ever be filled. I just want my mother, is that too much to ask? I just want my mom back in my life.

I keep thinking that, but no matter how much magic is in the Dove Pin I wear, it cannot bring people back from the dead. Why did I have to bring the world back to the way it is? Why couldn't I have just lived in that lie? Why was I so determined to return to a world like this.

My sobs are silent in the pillow I hide my face in as the night grows colder, and so does my soul in my sorrow. Everything feels empty right now, and I don't know if I will ever feel better about my decision to change things back to the normal world. Hopefully, in time, I will be able to get past this. Lifting my head from the now tear soaked pillow, I look over at my wall where a picture of my family hangs. I am only a baby in the picture, but both of my parents are there, as well as Nonna. My mother is holding me in her arms while sitting down in the garden in the backyard. My father is grilling something while Nonna is setting up some plates and such at a picnic table. It is a beautiful scene full of happiness, but that happiness is ruined when you know the truth behind that picture. That picture was taken only a week before my mom was put back in the hospital again, and a few days later she was gone. As I look at her smiling face, I feel the sobs coming back, and I bury my face in my pillow again, not wanting my remaining family members to wake up because of me. I want to suffer alone right now.

While the night goes on, I lie awake, wanting desperately to fall asleep, but the pain of my broken heart will not let me. Instead of having a peaceful night's rest after a fight, I stay awake wondering about all that I have lost so that I could win that battle.

Chapter Twenty- Two
Luis-
A New Plan
Emerges

It is late at night, but my lights are still on as I sit at my desk, thinking about everything that happened today. So many thoughts pass through my mind as I think of what needs to be done now that I have realized the truth. Several times though, as I try to think about my plan, my thoughts get invaded by memories of what that other world was like for me.

In that world I had an almost perfect life. In that world, I had something I have always wanted in my grasp. I was liked by everyone, no one made fun of me, Alex was getting teased instead and I was the one teasing him. It was everything I have wanted for almost my entire life, but one thing was wrong, I didn't have Colomba. Having her hate me was the thing that turned that dream into a nightmare. I gave up everything to have her be my friend again. I could have all the friends in the world, but that wouldn't mean anything if I didn't have her. She thought of me as a monster, and I can't live as a monster in her eyes. I suppose in that world I really was a monster though. I always complain in my mind about getting hurt and picked on, but I did it to someone else without a second thought just to get a bit of revenge. I actually feel guilty about this, I feel guilty about hurting Alex even though he has been doing that to me for years and has never said sorry. Why should I feel guilty about this when he never has? My heart aches a bit when I realize the answer to that question; I feel guilty because I want to be a better person than him, but I let myself sink to his level. I became the real bad guy at that moment. Why is it that when I finally get to feel good when it comes to Alex, it's wrong?

Looking down at my desk, I see the picture I have just finished sketching. In the picture, Demetrius is standing on top of his machine, ready to crush the school beneath him. Sighing softly, I flip through the pages of my sketchbook, my records of all the people I have transformed. In this book I see so many of my failures, my mistakes. I shouldn't have done all of this, there was a better way, there has been a better way since the very beginning. I should have seen that years ago. Putting the sketchbook back in my desk drawer, I lean back in my chair, resting my hands on my chest, trying to let my mind grow quiet so that I can think more clearly. A voice beside me interrupts my silence though.

"So you did it again?" I am not even surprised when I open my eyes to see Shadow perched on the arm of my chair, glaring at me with her black eyes. I must have placed my hand on the medal by accident. I pick myself out of the chair and slowly walk across the room to look into the mirror above my dresser. In the reflection, I can still see the fury in her gaze. "You promised me Luis, but you keep disappointing me! You said you wouldn't transform another person, and you did! You said you would start working with Silver Dove instead of trying to fight her! You lied to me! You almost lost everything in that world your little slave created!" I take in a deep breath, trying to calm myself so that I won't lash out at my good friend. Even though I am trying to calm myself down, Shadow only seems to get more upset as she speaks. "I told you that this wouldn't work, and to make things even worse, if Silver Dove hadn't solved this, you would have never gotten the Crow Medal back and you would have been stuck in a universe where Colomba would hate you! What do you think about your decision now?!" I can see Shadow staring up at me in the reflection of the mirror, but I don't turn around to face her, I just glare at her in the reflection. After a moment of my silent glaring, her dark expression cracks as a look of worry comes over her feathered face. "Luis?"

Her voice cracks in fear as she looks at me, and when I look in the mirror I can see why. A grim expression is on my face and a fire burns within my eyes that I have never seen before. I have been angry many times in my life, but this is a fury I have never felt before. Three years of disappointment and misery with my failures as the Crow seems to just crush me all at once as I face this most recent failure. As I look into my dark, burning eyes I think about each of my failures against Silver Dove one by one. I think of my first one when I attacked the school with my demon dogs and met her, I think of each soldier I have transformed, starting with Tigerclaw until this one today. I think about them all and as my mind becomes darker and darker as I feel a wave of depression come over me, a sudden thought brings light back into my mind, and I realize the obvious. The fire does not die in my eyes, but it changes. It is no longer a flame of rage, but a burning ambition. I glance back up at Shadow and her feathers fluff out a bit in discomfort as I smile coldly at her.

"Well Shadow, I have thought about my decision, and you were right. It was not the right thing for me to do, this was never the way for me to go." Even though I'm saying exactly what she wants me to, I know that she can tell that I have more to say because of my sarcastic tone. "Yes, I never should have made my soldiers to go after everyone in the school, I should have just gone after one person instead." Shadow's black eyes widen in terror, but I don't care. "I should have gone after Silver Dove from the start. If I just take her out, then the entire school will fall at my feet, and I can make all the pain end. I will control the school and make sure that nobody ever gets hurt again. When Silver Dove sees how great I make everything, then she will follow my lead too and help me keep everyone in line." Shadow seems too shocked to speak as she looks at me, as if she is seeing a completely different person, and when I look at myself, I can see why she sees that. As I look at myself, I see someone with a cold expression, like I am looking through myself instead of at myself. Within my eyes, I can't see anything, no emotion, just a dark nothingness. As I look within that nothingness, I feel myself smile, embracing the darkness I feel. Things are going to be a whole lot different very, very soon.

Don't miss the previous books in The Adventures of Silver Dove series. Check them out at elizascalia.com.

Eliza Scalia is a therapist who has a master's degree in Clinical Mental Health from Troy University. She enjoys reading, writing, and needlework. Eliza has been writing since she was in middle school and has self- published the Death's Assistant series for young adults. She lives with her husband Paul and her dog Lady.

9 781962 168472